"This moving and unsettling portrait of obsession run amok might have been written in 1970s Turkey, when social mores after Ataturk were still evolving, but it stays as relevant as the country struggles to save the very democratic ideals on which the Republic was rebirthed." — *Booklist*, Starred Review

". . . as Zeberjet becomes increasingly unhinged, we're drawn into his dark interior life while coming to understand Turkey's post-Ottoman uncertainty. Sophisticated readers will understand why Atılgan is called the father of Turkish modernism." — *Library Journal*

"An unsettling study of a mind, steeped in violence, dropping off the edge of reason." — *Kirkus Reviews*

"Yusuf Atılgan, like Patrick Modiano, demonstrates how the everyday can reflect larger passions and catastrophes. Beautifully written and translated, *Motherland Hotel* can finally find the wider audience in the west that it deserves." — Susan Daitch, author of *The Lost Civilization of Suolucidir*

"My heroes are Ahmet Hamdi Tanpınar, Oğuz Atay, and Yusuf Atılgan. I have become a novelist by following their footsteps . . . I love Yusuf Atılgan; he manages to remain local although he benefits from Faulkner's works and the Western traditions." — Orhan Pamuk

"*Motherland Hotel* is a startling masterpiece, a perfect existential nightmare, the portrait of a soul lost on the threshold of an ever-postponed Eden." — Alberto Manguel, author of *A History of Reading*

"Yusuf Atılgan gives us a wonderful, timeless novel about obsession, with an anti-hero who is both victim and perpetrator, living out a life 'neither dead nor alive' in a sleepy Aegean city. *Motherland Hotel* is an absolute gem of Turkish literature." — Esmahan Aykol, author of *Divorce Turkish Style*

Motherland Hotel

Motherland Hotel

A NOVEL

Yusuf Atılgan

Translated from the Turkish by Fred Stark

City Lights Books | San Francisco

Translation copyright © 2017 by the Estate of Fred Stark

Motherland Hotel was originally published in Turkish as *Anayurt Oteli* in 1973 by Bilgi, and is currently published by Yapi Kredi Yayinlari, Istanbul.

Library of Congress Cataloging-in-Publication Data

Names: Atılgan, Yusuf, author. | Stark, Fred, 1939-2013, translator.
Title: Motherland Hotel / Yusuf Atilgan ; translated by Fred Stark.
Other titles: Anayurt Oteli. English
Description: San Francisco : City Lights Publishers, 2016.
 Identifiers: LCCN 2016018905 (print) | LCCN 2016029637
(ebook) | ISBN   9780872867116 (paperback) | ISBN
9780872867123 (eISBN) | ISBN   9780872867123
 Subjects: LCSH: Single men—Turkey—Fiction. | Psychologi-
cal fiction. | BISAC: FICTION / Literary. | FICTION / Urban
Life. Classification: LCC PL248.A77 A8213 2016 (print) | LCC
PL248.A77 (ebook) | DDC 894/.3533—dc23
LC record available at https://lccn.loc.gov/2016018905

City Lights Books are published at the City Lights Bookstore
261 Columbus Avenue, San Francisco, CA 94133
www.citylights.com

Translator's Introduction

The appeal of *Motherland Hotel* to the Western reader should be two-fold. First, it presents small-town life in Turkey as something other than a long costumed vendetta. Second, there is a rare marriage of attitudes in the novel—oriental concern, even obsession, with pattern; intellectual assumptions recognizably European and 20th-century; and an "everyday-ness" (each culture has its own) which is thoroughly Turkish, or Aegean Turkish to be exact.

Exactness is the byword for this novel. As a precise study in mental disturbance it was for a time required reading for psychiatry students in Ankara's major hospital-university complex. As an exercise in strict purity of form—here that love of pattern finds expression—it came as a statement of artistic integrity at a time of political and social turmoil when very few writers in Turkey dared to veer from overt commentary. Not that *Motherland Hotel* is devoid of political implications, but they are implied, not brandished at the reader.

A few things we are assumed to know: Turkey was occupied by various foreign powers during and after the First World War. It was only through the passion and genius of Mustafa Kemal Atatürk that a militia was rallied and, against the heaviest continual odds, inspired to drive the occupying forces out. The "Liberation" referred to in the novel is the final push that ended on September 9, 1922, with the Greek army trapped in the bay at Izmir. The "Republic" is again the work of Atatürk. Given a base of near worship[1] by his war successes, he was able to impose Western-style democracy on a people who had known five centuries of autocratic rule under the sultans. Reforms in clothing, the alphabet and women's rights quickly followed, but of course the cultural patterns of half a millennium are not altered overnight. The extent to which Turkey has and has not freed itself from the past is, in fact, one of the background themes of *Motherland Hotel*.

As to the rest, the book will speak for itself.

Fred Stark
Ankara 1977

---

1. Which persists. This was brought home to the translator in a hotel one morning when honking horns and a loud siren made me think war was on. Then I noticed a plasterer down the hall standing at respectful attention. It was 9:05 a.m., November 10th, the anniversary of Atatürk's death in 1938, and it is with this minute of horns and sirens that the occasion is observed each year throughout Turkey.

FORMS OF ADDRESS

Men	*Women*	
bey	hanim	the mantle of money and position
abi	abla	literally, "big brother, big sister"; very widely used to show a familiar kind of respect
efendi		term of formalized condescension
agha		term of maximum respect *among peasants*
usta		title bestowed on the artisan (auto mechanic, plumber, etc.)

Thus a peasant named Kerim who settles in Istanbul to be an apartment-house janitor will refer to its residents as Bey and Hanim, as they will refer to each other while calling him Kerim Efendi. If he has to address a cop it will be as abi. All, however, is made up for at home, where his wife speaks to Kerim as agha.

Note that Agha as an actual title implies a kind of feudal overlordship, and as such has disappeared from western Turkey.

ZEBERJET, CLERK AT THE Motherland Hotel, let himself
into the room where on Thursday, three nights before, she
had stayed—the woman off the delayed train from Ankara. Turning the key and placing it in his pocket, he leaned
back against the door to survey the room. Everything was
just as she had left it: the quilt thrown back, the rumpled
sheet, the slippers, the chair, the reading lamp on the bedside table, two half-smoked cigarettes stubbed out in the
copper ashtray, the teapot, strainer, tea-glass and spoon,
the small dish with its five lumps of sugar (that night he
had brought her six Could I have some tea she'd asked and
he had brewed it in the three-serving pot then tray in hand
had knocked Come in she sat there on the edge of the bed
coat off black sweater necklace of large silver balls *she'd
looked up* Sorry for the trouble and asked how to reach that
village Then wake me at eight casually saying she carried
no ID. The next morning he had noticed the scent on entering and quickly shut the door. She had left the light on.
He'd taken note of the towel over the foot of the bedstead,
the thrown-back quilt, the rumpled sheet, the slippers, the
chair, the reading lamp on the bedside table, two half-
smoked cigarettes stubbed out in the copper ashtray, the
teapot, strainer and tea-glass, the small dish with its lumps
of sugar. Counting, "She takes one." But that scent was gone
now, perhaps was gone the night before, though ever since

her departure [setting down a small leather suitcase that morning to open her purse What does it come to Never mind the change no ring on Well thanks so much then for the tea too picked up her suitcase and left] the door had been locked and the key in his own pocket. Except that after waiting the whole day till midnight when all the guests were in, after locking and barring the main door [the bell had rung he'd opened she at the door coat unbuttoned suitcase in hand Do you have a room and he strode to the key rack] he'd been switching off the lobby light and coming here for three nights now), her towel forgotten on the foot of the bedstead, the gold-fringed maroon curtain, the sink and over it the round mirror (where the morning she had left he caught his face. Everything down-turned there—tips of eyebrows, corners of mouth, nose. He had studied the face, its small, square mustache; though he did shave three times a week This was the face she had looked at that night [easing down the tea tray, leaving to re-lock and bar the main door, he had set the alarm for six— though he always woke up at six—turned off the light and, clock in hand, had gone past her door, carefully treading the linoleum-covered stairs to the attic with its two rooms {the maid's room, rank with sweat. She sleeps a great deal, turns in early. Every morning he has to shake her awake. At night he'll come in as a rule and lie with her. To sleep undisturbed she beds with no underthings and with legs slightly apart. When he strokes her, even when he's on her, she goes on sleeping. Sometimes he'll bite a nipple and she mumbles "Ow" or "Scat." When he's through he climbs off and uses a handkerchief to wipe her dry} and had chosen his own room. He had set the clock within reach on the floor, undressed and gone to bed. A while later, when the bed shuddered from a car passing below, he sat up. He'd forgotten to wash his feet. Every night he washed them before bed. He got up, washed his feet, and came back. Sat on the edge of the bed for a time. "Suppose she hasn't locked the door. Someone could open it by accident." He dressed and went to the stairs, descended quietly, and stood beside her door. Keyhole dark. He held his breath listening, heartbeat painful. Slowly, pausing frequently, he turned the smooth round knob clockwise and tested the door with his shoulder. Locked. His breathing steadied and he turned the knob back, again slowly, again intermittently pausing, and let it go; then climbed deliberately up the stairs, went into the maid's room, and switched on the light. The quilt lay motionless. From under it poked her feet, big, the soles black. He snapped off the light and withdrew, shutting the door on his way out, then went back to his room and lay down fully clothed: awake all night long, alarm might fail, might sleep through] and the same face she had seen that morning. Toward eight he had put the kettle on the kerosene burner. At eight exactly he approached her door but paused to let her sleep the extra minute. Then knocked. "That's fine, I'm getting up." He brewed the tea, straightened his tie, sat down in his chair. The thick register lay before him. He could hardly ask her name now that she was about to leave. She had pulled her door shut and was coming toward the desk. Black hair, unbuttoned brown coat, smoke-gray stockings, low-heeled shoes. She set down the small leather suitcase to open her purse asking, "What does it come to?" Then, "Never mind the change." No ring on. Long, palely pink nails. "Well thanks so much then. For the tea, too." She picked up her suitcase and left. As she was going through the doorway that man came in, small leather suitcase in hand. His face looked boneless. "Do you have a room?" "Yes." "A good one if possible. The room that woman had, who just left." "She hasn't checked out, sir. She's staying on." "All right, another one then." He fished an ID from his pocket, the standard birth certificate booklet, and laid it on the hotel register. "Occupation?" "Put down retired officer." Zeberjet took a key from the rack and handed it across. "Room 2, second floor. On your left at the top of the stairs." For the past three days this man had spent his afternoons and evenings in a corner of the lobby, reading books and newspapers, smoking, glancing up whenever the door opened. After eleven p.m. he would go up to his room. Last night, as Zeberjet was emptying the ashtray at his side, the man had seemed to have a question. Tonight it had been asked. He had come in late and stopped on the way up, breathing the boozy licorice fumes of raki. Their eyes had met. "You looked better with a mustache." Was he being funny? That morning Zeberjet hadn't been able to bring himself to shave it off. He smiled. "Doesn't she ever leave her room?" "Who?" "You know, that woman the day I arrived. Friday morning as I came. . . ." "Oh, her. She's checked out, sir. Yesterday morning." "Checked out? Where was she going?" "I wouldn't know, sir. She didn't say.") with hand-stitched flowers at top and bottom, the hotel towel on a hook to the mirror's right, the lampshade at the end of a lead pipe that hung from the ceiling, the baroquely framed painting centered on the right-hand wall: a full-hipped, well-endowed woman all in lace reclining on a wide, highly ornate couch while two half-naked black girls stood on either side of her with fans. "A choice bit of harem-snatch," the Dentist had said. Zeberjet's father had brought it home from the flea market one day long ago and hung it up. "Son, when I'm dead and gone I don't want you giving this room to just anyone who comes along. Every hotel needs a room like this." He pulled himself away from the door and went over to the picture where he stood awhile looking. As he turned back toward the mirror there were stirrings from the room up above where that fellow was staying. He listened. Creak of floorboards, sound of water. 'Must be washing his face. Has he thrown up?' He looked at his reflection, mustached as usual, but with the effect of a slight tilt now to the nose. Turning again he went to the bedside. There were darkish stains on the pillowcase. What was she doing in that village? His knees felt shaky and he reached for the foot of the bed, but steadied and moved away. He left the bulb burning as he went out, locked the door, and headed upstairs. Some man was snoring in the double on the second floor. Putting out the hall light he stood by the door of Room 6 and listened. Not a sound. When he reached the top of the stairs to the attic there was a pair of eyes gleaming at floor level across from him. They belonged to the hotel cat.

The Town

or city. By day a westbound rail passenger, absorbed in the newspaper or chatting with his seatmate, when the train slows will wonder where they are and, glancing left, be startled. A mountain, its upper half sheer granite, is like a wave about to break over the train. The town (or city), with its minarets and broad, shady streets, spreads across the gentle slopes at the foot of this mountain. (The broad streets, parks and parade ground all date from the Fire. In early September of 1922 the Greek army had set this town to the torch before withdrawing. Old-timers say that if just one gunman in each neighborhood had shown his face, then nothing would have burned. Almost everyone fled to the mountain, where all that day and night they watched the great Fire.) A green and yellow plain stretches away north of the town. Along it flows a river, winding sluggishly in the summer months, murkily swelling in the winter. The plain boasts vineyards, cotton and wheat fields, and villages of some size.

The Hotel

is one of the buildings, spared the torch because wealthy Greeks had lived in the district, that stand opposite a street connecting the main avenue with the square behind the station. Three-stories, it was originally a manor house. (When Rüstem Bey of the Kecheji line—the "cloth-merchant" family—settled in Izmir after the Fire he turned his house into a hotel at the insistence of Ahmet Efendi, who was formerly a clerk with Vital Statistics. In time a washstand came to be installed in each room, a toilet on each floor. The lobby, halls, stairs and wooden flooring of the rooms were meanwhile being carpeted with linoleum. As the years went by and that small-town-hotel odor seeped into the walls and woodwork, Rüstem Bey's old manor house turned into a real hotel. According to him it had been his grandfather, Melik Agha, who built the house in the previous century. On the doorway arch now covered by the hotel sign there was supposed to be an inscription in relief on white marble. Conforming to neither classical nor syllabic meter—some local hack poet, cadging a livelihood by churning out rhymes whenever a death or birth among the town gentry required, must have hit a creative snag when the manor house was ready—the jingle etched into the stone under that sign was, as reported, somewhat odd:

One two and a double face
Kecheji's son Malik's place

In Arabic numerals one followed by two and then two circles reads twelve fifty-five; eighteen thirty-nine by the modern calendar.)

The front of the hotel on the avenue side is painted ochre. Three marble steps rise to a double door with their glass upper halves protected by iron bars. Flanking the door are two large windows, also barred—unlike those on the other floors. A tin sign hangs on the arch above the door, in white lettering on a dark green background: THE MOTHERLAND HOTEL. (An emblem perhaps of the shamefaced patriotic zeal to be found, during the years just after Liberation, in those towns and cities where very little had been done about the enemy.) Across from the door as you go in there is a stairway to the second floor with a carved wooden banister, and to its left a room that serves as a combination pantry, linen closet and tea galley. (In the village to which the woman off the delayed train from Ankara asked directions, Rüstem Bey had an acquaintance whose son, the same age as Zeberjet, used to stay in this room during the winter while in secondary and high school. Later, with Zeberjet in the army, his father had moved in down here, and in fact it was the handiest room for the clerk. But when his father died Zeberjet hadn't moved down. He kept his old quarters where at one time he had made a habit of reading library books and jerking off to visions of high school girls' gym class.) Between this cubicle and the foot of the stairs, a wooden armchair and a high half-moon-shaped desk stand on a platform. (The burly, loquacious dentist who stays for a couple of nights every year when the Party convention brings him from a distant county calls this Zeberjet Efendi's rostrum.) Next to this is a long, narrow table and on it, flush with the wall, an iron safe. Beneath the stairs a windowed door opens onto the back yard. The lobby has a pair of low square tables hedged round with black leather-upholstered armchairs, four to a table. Two lead pipes hang from the ceiling and end in lampshades. A full-length portrait of Mustafa Kemal Atatürk on the righthand wall, and just as you start upstairs, a door on the right bearing the numeral 1. Walls and doors alike are done in off white—paint, not limewash. To the right of the main door a rectangular placard: *Door Locked After Midnight*. One flight up on the left are a single and a triple, and on the right a double, a triple, and the toilet. The third floor is a replica of this. At each side of the three midway landings a window looks out onto the yard. The attic has a bathroom and kitchen on the right, and two slope-ceilinged rooms on the left with small lights and their view of the neighboring roof. In the enclosed yard, an open shed on the left runs along one of the three high stone walls. Here the maid does her weekly wash. If it's raining she drapes her sheets and other laundry over two thick lines strung the length of the shed. A large iron gate, rusty and discolored, opens from the yard onto a street. Next to the righthand wall are a stable and quarters for coachman and groom. (At the head of the street leading from the station square hangs a dark green tin arrow with HOTEL lettered in white, nailed to a pine tree. But one of the nails—eroded through over the years—has sheared off, so the sign points downwards giving the impression that the hotel lies underground.)

Zeberjet

Of not quite average height, but not particularly short either. In the army they had him listed at 5'4" and 119 pounds. Now, at the age of thirty-three, he could strip and weigh in at 124 or 5. For the past two years his stomach muscles have been going flabby. Head too large for his body, high forehead. Hair, eyebrows, eyes and mustache are brown. A pinched face, somewhat downturned but not, after all, as much as he found its reflection that morning, when the woman off the Ankara train had left. Small hands, stubby fingernails. Narrow shoulders and chest. He was born at seven months. Toward evening of November 28th, 1930, his mother had felt the pangs. After a while she saw there was no point trying to wait them out and put a scarf on to go down to the head of the stairs. "Ahmet Efendi," she called out, "go for the midwife." Who happened to be home so Ahmet Efendi reappeared shortly, midwife in tow. They had the mother lie in the righthand room. "Two months to go, midwife. Will I lose this one as well?" The midwife had turned to the expectant father. "You go boil some water." "So I locked the front door and put the water on. Your mother cried out maybe twice while it was heating, then the door opened a crack and the midwife asked for the water. 'It's a boy,' she said. Called me in soon after. She'd got you all swaddled and lying there in the palm of her hand. That's how small you were. 'You could wrap this one in cotton and lay him in a jewel-box,' she said. 'Call him Zeberjet—peridot.' So I leaned and whispered the name in your ear." A very rare name. There were four men from one of the provinces staying at the hotel that night, come to town because some relative was on trial. Returning from their supper out they had shaken Ahmet Efendi's hand and given the child their blessing.

During his mother and father's lifetime, Zeberjet had had this premature birth rubbed in on various occasions.

1. Morning. Ready for school, comes down to the lobby. His father there scooping clinkers out of the coal stove, which at that time they used for heat.

Zeberjet: Father, can you let me have twenty-five qurush?

Father: Any special reason?

Zeberjet: I have to buy a notebook.

His father loads clinkers into the bucket, then pokes the shovel back into the grate.

Zeberjet: Come on, Father, I'm late.

Father: Keep your pants on, son. Let me get these clinkers. How you managed waiting seven months to come out I'll never fathom.

2. Home from school one noon. Goes upstairs. His mother chopping lettuce onto a plate. There's a pot on the kerosene stove.

Zeberjet: I'm hungry.

Mother: It's almost ready, be patient. What a boy! Couldn't wait nine months to be born, even.

(If impatience did figure in this birth it could just as well have been on the part of the mother as the fetus in her womb. The former probability seems stronger. Expecting adult behavior from a fetus would be harsh. But a woman pregnant at forty-four might well be in a hurry, particularly if she has had three miscarriages; one at two months, another at two and a half, a third at three. Nevertheless, and whether the boy deserved these accusations or not, they had a positive effect on him. As he grew up, Zeberjet became progressively more serious and patient.)

The summer he graduated from elementary school brought his circumcision. Before that summer was over his mother died. His father didn't send him to secondary school, and for the next eight years, until he did his military service, the two of them ran the hotel together. Two months after Zeberjet's discharge his father died; put off dying until his son came back from the army, seemingly, to keep the hotel in family hands. Sixty-three years old, he died in his chair behind the tall half-moon desk one spring morning. Undertakers were found and they washed him in the back yard. After the burial the imam asked Zeberjet his grandmother's name. Not knowing, and declining to fabricate one (in view of possible complications above or here below) he simply lowered his gaze and blushed. "It's all right, my son," the imam had said, "a mother is a mother." Rüstem Bey got the telegram that night and arrived the next morning. He offered condolences, collected on arrears, and turned the hotel over to Zeberjet. "It's all yours," he said as he was leaving. "Make sure you get a woman in." "Did my father ever mention his mother's name?" "Not that I heard. Check his birth-certificate why don't you." "I've looked through his pockets and in the safe. There isn't any."

The Maid

Chestnut hair, deep blue eyes. A long face with a turned-up nose and toothy, full-lipped mouth. Medium height, firm and smooth-fleshed—what they call being "firm as a fish." Thirty-five years old and slightly bow-legged. Two years ago a man claiming to be an uncle showed up with her from a distant village. "Rejep Agha says you need a woman here." After some haggling over wages they sent her, bundle under one arm, upstairs. He asked the man to sit down for a glass of tea and as they sipped he listened to the woman's story. It seemed her mother and father were dead and that his family, the uncle's, had taken her in. At seventeen they had married her off but toward dawn of the wedding night the groom sent her back saying he wanted a virgin. "Well, then, little slut, who's been in at you? Dunno, she says, and won't tell. I beat her and so forth. I dunno, honest, is all she'll say. Lay off, says the missus, what's the difference anyhow?" Five years later they had given her to a widower with three children in a nearby village, and before three months were out he had brought her back because she slept too much. "She sleeps, she does sleep, but then she's hard working. Off in the village there's no peace for a divorced girl. No peace at all if she happens to be barren. Bachelors, married men, they all strut the mustache at her and watch for a chance. We heard from Rejep Agha the other day, so here we are. Now then, if you'll excuse me. . . ." He went and called up the stairs. "Zeeyy-*nep*! I'm leaving, you ill-bred goose, aren't you going to kiss my hand?" No answer. He shook his head. "All the best, then," and left. Zeberjet went up to the attic but didn't find her there. He searched the other floors. She had dropped her bundle in the middle of Room 2 and was sound asleep on the bed. He'd woken her up the next morning. She quickly got the hang of the routine. Always with her scarf on, she would make beds, swab floors, dust, cook every other day, launder on Sundays, and call Zeberjet "agha." But she didn't talk much. One day near the beginning as she was swabbing the stairs an old peasant came down from the third floor and she looked up. "Do you know the village of Sindelli, uncle?" "Sure do." "Pocked Ali is my uncle there." This uncle would come several times a year bringing a sack of milk curds, converse for a while, pocket her savings, and go away. "Should I give it to him—all your savings?" "Sure.

Sure, it's okay." An accounting would always be demanded down to the last qurush. "Five meters cotton flannel, money for seamstress, woolen vest . . . " "What's that? A woolen vest? She had a cotton one when she got here." It had been six years now since the uncle last appeared. (One early afternoon of the first week she'd been down on her knees swabbing the lobby floor. Zeberjet was in his chair reading the paper and at some point he looked up. She was leaning forward, bloomers stretched over her copious backside. Swabbing that way while slowly backing up gave it a motion, a certain rise and fall. He'd gone back to his paper, but from that moment on he'd seen her as a young female, up and about by day, asleep in the next room at night. On his way to bed he would pause outside her door and then have trouble sleeping. In dreams it would be army days again, the house in town with that tall woman. Often the two women would merge. Mornings when he went to wake her the room with its low, slanted ceiling always smelled. After opening the window he would stand at her bedside, shake her shoulders, and touch the breasts as if by mistake. One night he'd gotten up after going to bed and crossed to her room where he switched on the light. It was hot, and she was sleeping with no covers, and her shift was hiked up. He closed the door and went over, undid her buttons, took a breast in each hand, firm and full. He shook her. Not stirring she spoke in her sleep. "That you, uncle?" He shook her again. "Wake up girl, would you?" Her eyes opened and she rose in bed. "I'm getting up, agha." "Don't get up, just make room." Sliding over toward the wall, she saw Zeberjet's naked chest and jutting shorts. She turned her back and lay there. When he climbed in and rolled her over face up she closed her eyes. With some effort he took her bloomers off disclosing a thick patch. He lay on her and went ahead, panting and groaning. A short while later when he straightened up she looked very long, lying there, and he bent to listen. Her breathing was undisturbed.

The Woman Off The Delayed Train From Ankara

Twenty-six years of age, fairly tall. Chesty, with black hair and eyes, long lashes, eyebrows plucked somewhat. Sharp-nosed, thin-lipped, her face dark and taut.

The Man Claiming To Be A Retired Officer

Of medium height and stocky. Hair mostly gone to gray. Green eyes and bushy brows, a fleshy, thin-lipped face. The birth-certificate left on the register the morning of his arrival, and which was picked up again that same noon, gave his name as Görgün, Mahmut; his father's name as Abdullah, his mother's Fatma. It says he was born in Erzinjan, 1327 (1910 or 1911 by the modern calendar).

The Cat

Male, black. The second cat since Zeberjet took over. A tall girl in town with her father to see the ancient ruins, who stayed two nights and always carried a few horse-chestnuts in her purse, had christened the cat Lampblack. But nobody uses this name.

The Two Towels In The Room

1. The hotel towel. Hanging to the right of the mirror. Small, solid green. One slightly crooked 'M' and one

straight 'H' are sewn in white thread into one corner, with a vague dot between them. Added by Zeberjet to prevent theft after three other towels had been taken. Only a single towel had been taken during his father's time (thirty years), whereas the ten years that Zeberjet has been in charge have seen a total of nine towels and two pairs of slippers carried off. His father had made that one incident the basis for a fulminating indictment of mankind, which he maintained was made up entirely of thieves. Actually, the possible causes for increased theft at the hotel may be ranged by a tranquil mind as follows:

a) There may be more thieves around.

b) More people may enjoy rebelling against traditional values—honor, decency, etc.

c) Something about Zeberjet's father may have intimidated potential filchers. (This is the weakest likelihood. When Zeberjet was sixteen and still waiting for a mustache, Rüstem Bey, who used to come in from Izmir every month to collect the hotel proceeds, had stroked his hair once and called him a "drop off the old cock.")

2. The towel forgotten by the woman off the Ankara train. Tossed over the foot of the iron bedstead, half trailing onto the quilt. The towel has broad red and yellow stripes, narrow black ones.

MONDAY

He woke to a dim room. From on top of the chest of drawers at his bedside he took a heavy Omega pocket watch that had been given to his father (while still a clerk at Vital

Statistics) by a friend as collateral against the loan of two gold pieces. He held it to the window—quarter of six—wound it, put it down. The front of his underwear was jutting and he pushed it down with his left hand, then sat up, sniffed his undershirt, and got out of bed. Before going to the john he set some water on the kerosene stove and when he was out he bathed, dried off, wrapped a towel around himself and went back to the room. He took some clean things from the chest of drawers, put them on, combed his hair in a small mirror on the wall. Mustache per usual. Tucking the watch into his vest pocket he opened the window, made his bed, and dropped his socks and towel in the bathroom. Then to the maid's room. Opened the window, woke her up.

Downstairs he lowered the iron bar from across the front door, took the key out of his lefthand pocket, undid the lock. In the pantry he boiled water in the two-serving pot, brewed himself some tea, and laid out breakfast on a tray. Toward seven he was at the desk eating. Tea with his normal one lump. There were knockings and creakings upstairs, and a middle-aged peasant with a bushy mustache came down. Zeberjet had asked the night before. He was not from that village.

"Enjoy your breakfast."

"Join me?"

"Thanks anyway. What do I owe?"

He paid up and left. Zeberjet was picking at his food. After one more glass of tea he cleared the tray, brushed his teeth, and went back to his chair where he lit a cigarette. For the last three days he'd been smoking occasionally without inhaling. Had he smoked on Friday as well? Friday was muddled. While the man who called himself a retired officer read the papers after lunch Zeberjet had dozed off for a spell and woken to a tap on the desk. He had looked up to see a young couple all smiles. Had he been snoring? These were the married teachers newly assigned to the high school who had checked in on Tuesday. They planned to stay until they could rent a place of their own. "Feeling unwell?" "No, just a headache."

He laid his cigarette in the ashtray, opened the register in front of him, and began making entries from yesterday's forms in a hand that was legible, if cramped. The register had two days per page, each day with numbers from 1 to 9 and laid out according to beds per room. He turned back to Thursday. Twelve names, but nothing for the room where the woman off the delayed train from Ankara had stayed. It didn't really matter, seeing that he gave the room to only a few guests each year, and that every other week he would show a bed or two unoccupied to account for the lira-per-day that went—each morning when he availed himself of a lull to stow the drawer cash in the safe—from the hotel funds into his own. But he wanted to establish her having been there, in that room, that night. Still, he couldn't just put down a name.

He closed the register. His cigarette had gone out. Side by side, two men were coming down the stairs. They were livestock dealers who stayed at the hotel now and then. They paid and were on their way out when he all but asked them. No. Better go to the barber. In putting away the cash he banged the wart on his left middle finger against the drawer. He had made it bleed the morning before, trying to pick it off with his nail. He pushed the drawer closed. The clock on the safe showed a quarter to eight. That fellow had said eight fifteen. He wound the clock and put it back. Down the stairs came the maid on her way out to shop. He made a list. Four eggs, two packs of Yenijé brand cigarettes, four boxes of matches. From his pocket he drew the broad leather wallet left him by his father and removed a fifty-lira bill. This, together with the list, he handed across.

"Add that to the groceries."

Her hands were purple from yesterday's laundry. Had she noticed? He couldn't tell. As she left, the trio of young men came down from Room 3, wooden suitcases in hand. Two of them had trim mustaches, the other was clean-shaven. Zeberjet had learned the night before that they were headed for their hitch in the army. They laughed and wisecracked over who should pay, then settled separately and left.

The maid, back from the grocer's, laid out his change along with the cigarettes and matches. Her string bag held two loaves, and before going upstairs she deposited one of these in the pantry. Zeberjet got out of his chair. He stretched his legs in the lobby for a while. At eight fifteen he went up to the third floor and stopped at Room 6. He could hear movement inside. This was the teachers' room. He knocked.

"That's fine, we're awake."

"That's fine, I'm getting up," she'd said that morning. This evening was too soon to expect her back. He went down and sat in his chair. People generally didn't come in for rooms during the morning. Any large vehicle passing outside on the avenue rattled the panes and shook the building. When the diesel thrum of the Izmir-Ankara train reached him the high school teachers were on the stairs hurrying down. They rushed out with a "Good morning." Only the self-styled Retired Officer was left upstairs. He always came down toward noon. For some reason Zeberjet felt that he'd be leaving today.

The front door opened. It was the newsboy, who left a paper. Every Monday Zeberjet gave him the week's check-in forms for delivery to the police station. He opened the righthand drawer now and rummaged a bit.

"Couldn't you pick them up tomorrow?"

"Okay. See you."

"So long."

He browsed through the paper for a while. Serap was nervous today, wary of her john. A prostitute with drooping shoulders, Serap (she had other names) sometimes brought men to the hotel. Folding and laying aside the paper, Zeberjet opened the cash drawer, then took the key from his inside pocket to unlock the safe. There were two compartments. In the upper one, along with receipts and two birth-certificate booklets, was an envelope marked HO-TEL into which he now slid the cash. From the small copper change bowl he took one lira and put it into a similar bowl in the lower compartment. One of the two envelopes in this lower compartment was marked ZEYNEP. From the other, a thick one marked ME, he withdrew a pair of five-hundred-lira bills. Then he swung the door shut, locked it, replaced the key in his pocket, and took out the wallet. The two five-hundreds went in alongside several hundreds, then he folded the wallet and put it back in his pocket, which he patted with his left hand. He sat down, and dipped into his breast pocket for the fiver that the woman off the Ankara train had given him. This he smoothed out on the register. Not exactly given him. She had paid with two tens and said never mind the change. That morning, after spending some time in her room, he had withheld the five from the bills going into the safe. He creased the note double now and tucked it back into his pocket.

Toward noon the Retired Officer came downstairs. Under his usual sports jacket he wore a pale green sweater. No suitcase, which meant he was staying. Passing the desk he half turned to offer a greeting, face clean-shaven as usual. He shut the front door softly on his way out.

At noon the maid brought his lunch on a tray together with the keys.

"Did you swab the floor in Room 2?"

"Yes."

"Sheets clean?"

"All clean."

He hung the keys up. The numbers were etched into the metal. He ate without appetite, went to the pantry to wash his hands and lips, came back. Lit a cigarette, coughed. The maid was coming for the tray. Her own meals were taken upstairs in the kitchen. Stubbing out his cigarette he heard the 1:10 train pull in. Outdoors the woman took yesterday's wash off the line and carried it to the pantry. When she started ironing it was past 1:30. No one was coming, he got up. At the door of the room he stopped.

"I'm going out for a while. If anyone asks for a bed say yes."

"All right."

He looked around. Everything in place. Then he opened the front door and went out. The weather was fine, just a cloud or two. He headed downtown. Naturally he couldn't go to the neighborhood barber on the street leading to the station. This wasn't his day there. Once every four weeks on Thursday afternoon the barber would send his apprentice to the hotel when no one was waiting to call Zeberjet over for a haircut. Anyway, if he told his longtime barber to shave the mustache off there'd be no end of remarks. He'd go to one of the places on the avenue that led downtown. He seldom left the hotel. Unless something came up, as now, it was once a year or once every two years for the tailor, once in six months to have his dead skin cells scrubbed off at the Turkish bath, every four weeks a haircut, and once a month the post office where he would send the hotel proceeds to Faruk Kecheji who now lived in Istanbul. He paid the taxes once a year, but since this too was done at the post office it didn't require an extra trip. Whenever he went out, and especially at the Turkish bath, he felt apprehensive about the hotel. Now too he was hurrying, another reason for which was. . . .

"Hello. Where are you off to?"

The Retired Officer was coming back with today's newspapers.

"Going downtown is all."

He kept walking, past the pine trees and the high school, and came out onto the avenue. Each year the big vacant lots were filling up with more office and apartment buildings. The banks and department stores looked busy. On the corner of Printers Street there was a three-chair barber shop with two chairs vacant. As he stepped in, the elderly, gray-mustached barber got up from the corner. "Come right in," he said, holding a chair. Zeberjet sat down and looked in the mirror. There was the trim, square mustache. Wrapping the top of a cloth around his customer's neck the barber began snipping.

"Live around here?"

"No, I'm in town on business."

"Shall I cut it short?"

"No."

Next to him a young apprentice was following the haircut. The barber said something Zeberjet didn't catch. He laid his head back, eyes closed, for the soap to be lathered on. The razor slid over his cheeks, his throat, his chin, and came to his upper lip.

"Zip off the mustache, too."

The barber laughed. "You're quite the kidder," he said.

Two fingers held Zeberjet's nose while the razor did a thorough job on his lip. When he opened his eyes the mustache was gone. Now there was a hint of lift to his eyebrow tips, the corners of his mouth, and his nose. The barber guided Zeberjet's head forward over the sink and washed his face, then, after drying it, reached for a small can.

"No talcum."

He stood up for the apprentice to brush off his shoulders and collar. From the upper pocket of his coat came the five-lira bill, which he handed to the barber.

"Never mind the change."

Half an hour later behind a screen in a men's clothing store he stood before a tall narrow mirror propped against the wall, emptying the pockets of his old coat and observing his reflection in black slacks, a light blue sweater, and a black three-button sports jacket, all chosen with the attentive aid of the young salesman. In the righthand pocket he put his handkerchief and the key to the room where the woman off the Ankara train had stayed; in the lefthand pocket the front door key, the matches, and his pack of cigarettes; and in the inside pocket the key to the safe along with his pen-knife, which was chiefly used to pare his nails. The broad leather wallet didn't fit this pocket, although he could have forced it in. But he transferred the bills to his back pocket while the wallet went back into its old pocket in the other coat. Loose change into the left pants pocket. Then he removed the watch from his vest fob. The slacks had none, and at any rate the watch would have been too big. What was he going to do with it? For the time being he slid it into the righthand inside pocket. There was a small package on the chair containing a pale green duplicate of the blue sweater he was wearing. A last look in the mirror to straighten the hem of his jacket, and he came out from behind the screen. The salesman was beside him immediately, adjusting the collar of the sweater and undoing the upper and lower jacket buttons.

"That's it. Very becoming. Black shoes would be just the thing."

"What does it all come to?"

"You can pay the cashier. I'll wrap the old things for you."

Shortly after, he left with a package under one arm and walked past a bank, a baklava shop, a tailor's and a drugstore, then turned into a store where rows of footwear were stacked in a window display. He settled on a pair of black loafers. As they seemed to fit well enough, he had his old brown pair wrapped. He paid and went out. Stepping off the curb with his package and crossing the street, he heard a squeal—froze, and saw the car stopped with a few feet to spare. The driver smiled, shaking his head, and Zeberjet smiled back. "Sorry," he said. Passersby had stopped to smile with them. He hurried on. A sweet whiff of danger—but how easy it was, after all, to die.

Back to the hotel the way he had come. As he walked in his eyes met those of the Retired Officer, who was reading a newspaper in the corner. The maid was in the pantry ironing.

"Anyone been in?"

"Three boys. They left their luggage."

Crossing through he avoided looking at the Retired Officer. Three suitcases stood under the stairs. Up in the room he unwrapped his package on the bed. In the wardrobe at the foot of the bed he hung jacket and slacks, while the shoes, stuffed with paper, went underneath beside his others. The new pale green sweater he hung on the wall

33

rack. Then he looked in the mirror. "Quite the kidder," the barber had said. That didn't completely resolve it, but what mattered was the result. His mustache was gone. He took the watch from his inside pocket—almost three-thirty—and laid it on the edge of the chest. The downstairs alarm clock would do for the time being. Folded up, the wrappings were left in the bathroom. He took a long, drawnout piss. Downstairs again, he sat in his chair. The Retired Officer was regarding him.

"You look younger."

"Thanks, sir."

He took up the newspaper on the desk to avoid conversation. The corn on the little toe of his right foot hurt from the new shoe. Quietly he took the shoes off and wiggled his feet. He'd forgotten to ask for wart remover. It did look smaller, though. There was a family of wart-witchers in that village. He re-shod his feet. The maid, her ironing done, closed the door of the pantry and walked toward the stairs without looking at him. When the Retired Officer lit a cigarette Zeberjet followed suit. Gulped back a cough. Tonight he'd look in the ashtray. It was quiet in the hotel. Outside, the sound of cars and footfalls; inside, the ticking alarm clock.

Around five o'clock he leaned over to the wall and switched on the lights. The Retired Officer stirred, abandoning his paper for a book. It was getting to Zeberjet the way he sat there every afternoon and evening. Being alone had its advantages, such as getting up now and then as he used to and strolling around the lobby, or picking his nose—not often—when need be, or shifting to one side for a good loud fart, or, when his butt got sweaty, standing to fan it with the seat of his pants; none of which he could do now. He had been inconspicuous about taking his shoes off, had fought back a cough. Few people ever sat in the lobby. Sometimes five or six actors in a touring company would lodge at the hotel and spend time there after the performance, sitting around for shop talk, gripes over pay, and plain argument amid the cigarette fumes. Zeberjet would make tea for them. Usually these groups included two women. One actress had complained on a certain night of having to play three parts. Then there were the political conventions, when five or six county delegates would sit in the lobby and caucus. If the talk heated up, some important name would be invoked, followed by a "shussshh" and general glancing in Zeberjet's direction. Since the open conversation always had to do with matters of common knowledge, it seemed the genuine running of the country was in these whispers. On one occasion, when the dentist. . . .

The door opened and they both looked over. It was one of yesterday's livestock dealers.

"We'll be staying on tonight. Anyone take our room?"

"No, it's free."

The man paused in turning and peered at Zeberjet's face.

"You've shaved off your mustache."

"It was getting to be a weight," he said with a laugh and then, in an undertone, asked, "Did I have it this morning?"

"Can't say as I noticed," replied the man, who then left.

Which meant that the problem of the mustache had no ready solution. In fact there had been no point asking. A firm "yes" or "no" would still have failed to clear up the matter. Taking a form from the drawer he put the livestock dealers down for Room 5. Then he lit a cigarette and watched the Retired Officer, who sat with a book held close up in his right hand. Zeberjet smoked his cigarette through, watching. Not once was a page turned. Saturday evening on the way out he had drifted over for a peek. The book wasn't in Turkish.

As the maid was bringing supper in, the Retired Officer rose and went out, leaving the book on top of the newspapers. Supper was the same as lunch, but Zeberjet ate with relish. He carried his tray up himself, since after serving the maid always went straight to bed. He let the cat out of the kitchen, which he locked. Coming down he heard the 6:40. Emptied the ashtrays into the wastebasket. Paced for a time between the front door and the stairs. At the door to her room he stopped, put his hand to the round knob, then snatched it back as the main door opened. He turned to see the teachers.

"You're all dressed up tonight. Expecting a visitor?" asked the woman, laughing.

"Our things have arrived," said her husband. "We're leaving tomorrow, so I'd like to pay."

"Why not wait till morning?"

"No, let's settle now. We might have to hurry."

He took a five-hundred from his back pocket and laid it on the register. Going behind the desk Zeberjet opened the safe. Rooms with double bed were 15 liras for a single guest, 20 for a couple. He counted out change from the hotel envelope and re-locked the safe, then handed across their room key. The woman took it. No nail polish.

"Could you wake us at eight, please? Good night."

"Good night."

As the woman went up the stairs she slipped an arm through his. They both carried small leather satchels. She had a round bottom and good legs. He looked away and took up a pen to begin filling in their forms. Saïdé was her name. The same name as his mother. That had startled him

Tuesday when they checked in. Thursday night. . . . The door opened framing two middle-aged men in caps. Peasants, by the look of them.

"Got two beds?"

"Yeah."

He put them in one of the two triples on the second. Room 4.

"Where you from?"

"Kepekli," said one.

Not the same village. He gave them a key.

"At the far end, on the right at the top of the stairs. First door on the right is the john. Don't lock your door. I might have to put someone in with you."

They went up. Sometimes three total strangers would find themselves rooming together. Three years before he had come down one morning to an open front door. Whoever it was had made off with all the money his roommates were carrying, and their watches. This had occasioned one of his rare exits from the hotel, for ten days after the theft he'd been summoned to court as a witness. At the judge's question he at first had barely recognized the accused. But beneath the cowed and broken look it was the same man, youthful, medium tall, with a narrow swarthy face. Sometimes going up to the attic at midnight Zeberjet would hear the voices of two or three men conversing quietly in the rooms. He yawned. He picked his left nostril with his left pinky, considered the resulting bit of dry snot, and wiped it off under the chair. He wrinkled up his face. At the sound of the diesel train from Ankara he glanced at his watch. Almost on time tonight. He rose and went to put water on the kerosene burner in the pantry. When he had the tea steeping he came out to see a pair of men enter the lobby. One of them he recognized, a county lawyer.

His companion was elderly and well-dressed. They carried satchels, and were possibly back from litigation in Ankara.

"Do you have a double room?"

He took a key from the rack and presented it.

"Room 9 on the third floor."

While these two were still on the stairs the livestock men arrived looking sullen. He gave them their key. Then the Retired Officer came in, closing the door softly behind him before walking over.

"Has anyone asked for me?"

"No, sir."

He hadn't been drinking. After collecting his newspapers, book and key, he went up with a parting "Good night." Was Zeberjet imagining it, or was he waiting for her? He drank two straight glasses of tea. It was past ten-thirty now. Some time after eleven three young men came in, the ones who'd taken a room while he was out. He wrote their names down and asked while handing them the key. They were from Afyon, going into the army. Had just been to a movie. Retrieving their luggage from under the stairs they went up. Before long the bumping overhead had ceased. He lit a cigarette, stubbed it out half-smoked. It wasn't midnight yet, but no one would be coming. He locked and barred the front door, turned off the lights, and took the key to Room 1 out of his righthand pocket. Once inside he closed the door. The light was on, everything was just as she had left it. On the hook to the right of the bed. . . . What had she gone to that village for? Of all the possible answers going through his mind these past four days, the likeliest was that she had a brother who had been assigned to teach school there. At the most she'd be gone a week. Then, one evening on the 6:40 train, she'd come back to spend another night. Here. In her room. He moved

38

toward the copper ashtray to inspect the two half-smoked cigarettes. Their brand was unclear. Stopping his hand in mid-reach Zeberjet turned and left the room. The key, after being used to lock the door, went back into his right-hand pocket. He climbed up the stairs carefully, to avoid creaking. The lights in the corridors were all on. Pausing at the dark keyhole of Room 6 on the third floor he heard muffled voices from within. He cocked his head to listen, as he had on Saturday. Last night it had been silent. "Ah . . . hold tight . . . aah." The woman. The man's voice came too, but thick and indistinct. Face taut, mouth half open, eyes squeezed shut. "Yes, yes, till morning . . . ah, hold me always, don't let . . . ahh . . . how I'm yours." A sudden creak inside and he straightened to walk away, climbing slowly up the stairs. Across from him shone a pair of eyes. The cat. As Zeberjet entered the bathroom it rubbed up against him. He aimed a kick but missed. Turning on the tap he gave his face a long wash.

TUESDAY

He woke to a dim room, took his watch from the edge of the dresser and held it to the window. Five of six. He wound the watch, set it down, then drew his arms back in under the quilt. He poked stiffly through the slit of his underwear. He pressed it with his left hand, then gave the crown a flip with his finger. (It had been his first visit to the house in town, near the base. Corporal Halil had taken him. They had a pair of lower bunks in the barracks, side by side. During the first months they were always being rousted for middle-of-the-night guard duty, the most miserable. He never complained, but Corporal

Halil would bawl at the sergeants. To avoid any MPs they had approached the house via the empty lot in back and climbed in through a window, fairly high up. It had been opened by a gap-toothed woman well along in years. Corporal Halil had gone in first, hauling Zeberjet up by the arm. Five or six half-nude women in makeup were sitting and standing around in the parlor. A tall one spoke up in a casual, toneless voice. "Say, here's my little soldier." Another one sat on Corporal Halil's lap. "Go on up with her if you want," he said. On the narrow stairs Zeberjet could feel her thigh and hip. His heart was pounding. "I'll be right back," she said when they got to a small room, "you undress and lie down." He stripped hastily and sat on the far side of the bed. Stiff as a rod, the thing was pointing toward his navel. It occurred to him to put his briefs on but just then the woman came back. She had on a pink slip that fell to her knees, its lower half embroidered. A generous helping of her large breasts was on view. "Well look at that," she said, approaching. "It's about as big as the rest of you.")

He sat up and got out of bed, went to the bathroom and came back. While dressing he hesitated between the two sweaters, then chose the pale green. He combed his hair and opened the window. After making his bed he went over to the maid's room, but paused in opening her door. There was no cooking today. She had nothing to do but clean up the rooms. For the first time in ten years he let her sleep.

He took the breakfast tray into the pantry and brushed his teeth. Back in his chair again he opened up the register to begin making entries from last night's forms. Finishing with the second floor he came to Room 6. She was to be woken at eight. The woman reminded him of his fifth grade teacher. Young and gentle. Muhittin the Kurd, a boy who sold *simits* out on the street before coming to school in the morning, had nicknamed him "Seedless." The principal had come into class one day and given the boy a beating. This same boy had made up a rhyme to taunt him with. Muhittin used to sing, "His mother thought she bore a son, but Zeberjet kneads buns." He wrote down the name of the woman in Room 6, wondering what the fifth grade teacher was teaching now, and how the older boys could pay attention. Saïdé. Zeberjet's mother had been frail. She'd been born in this house, in what was now Room 6, and apparently her own mother had died shortly after the birth. As for her father, a relative of the Kechejis, he was supposed to have run off. She might even have been illegitimate, the issue of Rüstem Bey's father and one of the semi-adopted servant girls. It seems that Hashim Bey never let these girls alone. Even when he was past sixty, the one who brought coffee to his room (and whose place at night was in the attic beside Kadriye the Chief Maid) would get her breasts and bottom pinched. She had kept quiet about it until one day he forced her down onto the big cushion and she finally called for help. His daughter-in-law was the first to come running, and handled the situation with dismayed respect. Later on, unconstrained senility overtook him. Seeing a woman, he would take out his huge puckered member and beckon to her, "Don't be shy, sweetheart. After all, we're married." They locked him up in what was later to become the third-floor bathroom, and that's where he died.

Someone was moving around upstairs. He wrote down the names for Room 9 and shut the register. Registers from previous years were stored in a chest under the stairs together with some thick history books of his father's, printed in the old Arabic script. Once Zeberjet was out of grade school his father had taught him this script. "You'll learn fast. It only took me ten days to get the new alphabet down." Zeberjet's father had been a clerk with Vital Statistics. During the War of Liberation he had not been mobilized. He hailed from Adana, where his own father ran a hotel on lease. One day during school hours the hotel had collapsed in a mild earthquake. Father and mother, little brother and sister, all had died in the ruins. After school, he had stayed with his aunt for a while and worked at a hotel before going over to Statistics. After leaving Adana and settling in his new town, he had prepared the birth-certificate entry and booklet for Rüstem Bey's third daughter. The two men became acquainted, and sometimes they would play backgammon in the café at night. A third party had arranged the marriage. One evening there was an invitation to dinner at the manor house, and they had opened a door just enough to give a glimpse of the woman who was to be Zeberjet's mother. He had assented, and a year before the Greeks came they were married. She was twenty-two at the time, he thirty-eight.

At eight he woke the teachers and in another half hour they came down.

"We'll send for our luggage. It's been a very nice week in your hotel. Goodbye."

"Goodbye, sir."

The man put out his hand and Zeberjet shook it, but didn't look at the woman's face in shaking hands with her. She had plump fingers. When she let go he put his hand behind him. Was it sweaty? The man laid a ten on the desk.

"You forgot to charge for the tea yesterday."

They had asked for tea in their room on Sunday. Sitting across from one another at the table when he went up, they'd been correcting papers.

"That was on the house. No charge."

"Thank you."

He watched them leave. At night she had said, "How I'm yours." There must be other women on earth who talked to their men that way. Wanting a cigarette, he reached in the righthand pocket by mistake.

As he was stretching his legs in the lobby with everyone but the Retired Officer gone, the newsboy arrived. Zeberjet went to his desk and took the forms from their drawer to hand over. Thus the fact that the woman off the delayed train from Ankara had stayed in Room 1 on Thursday night went undocumented. He had racked his brains for nothing all this time. Any woman's name would have done, really. But only if she gave it herself. Before three days were out she'd be back to do that. He sat down and was about to reach for the newspaper when he changed his mind, opened the drawer instead, took out the cash and went over to open the safe. There was a single lira left in the upper bowl. He transferred this coin to the lower one and then switched the bowls, after which he took a ten and a five from the sheaf of bills in his hand and put them in his back pocket. The rent went into the hotel envelope and he shut the safe. There were footsteps on the stairs. At the landing, with its window facing the back yard, the maid stopped with face averted.

"What happened, agha?"

"Nothing happened. You were worn out yesterday so I let you sleep. Tidy up the rooms and change the sheets in 6."

She came down and got some sheets from the pantry. As she was passing him she hesitated and looked up before going on toward the stairs. Maybe she had noticed. The handkerchief under her pillow would be enough.

In the lobby that afternoon as they sat reading (not that he read much, really. A headline or two, a few un-comprehended lines of print—the newspaper was a blank to him) the door opened and they both looked up. It was someone for the luggage. Zeberjet took the key off its hook and showed the man upstairs. The room was bright, with the gold-fringed maroon curtain pulled back. She had left hers drawn, and forgotten to turn off the light. "These things must be full of bricks," said the man. They went out and Zeberjet opened the main door for him. Coming back to sit down he took up the paper. If she arrived on the 6:40 the Retired Officer would be out. But she might come before then, since *dolmushes* had been making runs to the village and back for the last five or six years. It was a large village, nearby on the plain. When his father was alive he'd gone there once on a summer's day when he was fifteen, invited by Ömer; "Just ask where the Black Mustafas live." She must have gone through that same square too, with its fountain. The men sitting out in front of the cafe would stare. In a long vineyard they'd eaten sweet-smelling grapes and they had fished in the Kumçay. There were oxen lying in their path and Ömer had skipped across on their backs, without the beasts even stirring. Zeberjet, shoes and pants in hand, had taken the long way around while Ömer and the herdsman laughed. It was the final year of the war, when bread was scarce. That evening as he was leaving they had wrapped him a home-baked loaf, fresh from the backyard oven. Was it 6:40 so soon? He looked over where the Retired Officer had his face in the paper. One reason the man got on his nerves might be that he was a former officer. "Zeberjet, son of Ahmet!" "Yes, sir." "Pipe down, we're not deaf in here." After six months in that company the captain had made him his orderly, having asked one day what he did in civilian life. There was another hotel clerk, but the captain picked Zeberjet. The house was a large one, with a room just off the entryway where he slept. All morning long like a maid. . . . The captain's wife and her aged sister would talk freely when he was there, paying him no attention. Once a month when they went to the Turkish bath he would carry the bundle and wait at a cafe across the street for them to come out. The cafe owner and his helper would tease him. "Four glasses of strong tea for the ladies." "Who's going to take it in, you?" "I should live so long. With that stew-faced biddy at the door?" "Look at him blush, would you? Come night time. . . ." The women always took their two little sons along. The smaller baby-talked, called him Gebejet. Zeberjet's father never knew he was an orderly. The reason he gave for using the home address of a friend was that mail received through company channels was opened. Zeberjet's letters were almost all alike. He often asked for money: his rifle barrel would get pitted, or his canteen stolen, or his bayonet would break. Once or twice a week he'd pay an afternoon visit to the brothel, going around behind, where it was always that gap-toothed older woman who opened the window. "It's for you, girl," she would call. "Here's my little soldier." And they'd pull him through by the arms. Sometimes his regular would be upstairs with someone and he'd have to sit and wait. "She's been at it a while, cousin." They'd all have a laugh. He never knew which of the men going up and down had been the one. When she finally came down she'd speak in a listless tone that failed to match her words. "Here's my little soldier."

"What was that?"

He caught himself and answered: "Nothing, sir."

While he was eating supper he noticed the maid by the staircase, leaning against the banister and waiting.

"Go on upstairs and sleep."

She bowed her head and made no answer. He was rushing his meal. The beans were overcooked.

"There was a dish you made with corn flour. Why don't you try that again?"

"You mean *kachamak*? All right."

He went to the pantry with the uneaten bread, which he put in a pan, then washed his lips and looked in the mirror. He brushed his teeth once again and walked out, shutting the door. Before taking away his tray the maid wiped off the desk. He sat down and lit a cigarette. How many did that make? He had gotten over coughing. Outside, footsteps went by now and then. He was putting out his cigarette when he heard the train. "Hello, is my room free? Is my room free? Is the room free? Hello, is the room free? Is my room free? Is the room free? Is there a vacant . . . ? Hello, is there a vacant? Good evening, is there a vacant room? Good evening, is my room free? Hello. . . ." He shook himself and stood up to straighten his jacket and then came round to the front of the desk, on which he rested his right hand, waiting. He counted backwards from a hundred to thirty-three. There was no need to panic. She might not even come tomorrow. He withdrew his hand from the desktop and went over to empty the Retired Officer's ashtray. As he was replacing it the door opened and two men came in, one middle-aged, the other youthful.

"Do you have a double room?"

"Yes."

He went to the desk and asked for their IDs. The older man took both from his pocket and showed them. The last names matched.

"Room 5 on the second floor. Shall I give you the key now?"

"No, we'll come back later."

They left. Until the recent past, Zeberjet had given the clientele little scrutiny. Anyone who wasn't blind drunk could have a bed. He'd pretend not to recognize the prostitutes who showed up sometimes playing man-and-wife with a customer, and would give them a double bed in Room 2 or 6, where actual married couples stayed. As for the young men who occasionally appeared with their middle-aged (and usually ill-at-ease) "fathers" or "uncles," he let them have rooms with twin beds. These husband-wife, father-son and uncle-nephew pairs were quiet and always left early in the morning. But he'd been leery of male couples ever since an incident five months before. One night in mid-May an elderly man had come in rather late with a sweet-looking young blond boy. "Have you got a double room?" He'd written down the names they gave and presented the key. "Second floor, Room 5 on the right." When, after turning the lights off around midnight and climbing the stairs, he had paused by their door to listen, the conversation ("that's right . . . and his") had been unintelligible. He had continued on up to the attic, undressed, and gone into the maid's room. As he was lying down someone had cried out below, twice. By the time he rushed into his clothes and hurried down the whole hotel was up, with five or six men collected at the door of Room 5 in their underwear. "It came from in there." "Should we break in?" "Let's call the police. Isn't there a phone somewhere?" "Here's the hotel-keeper," said one of them, "make way." Knocking, he had asked through the door, "Did you call out?" "It's all right, the boy was having a nightmare." "Do you take us for idiots?" someone said. "Please open this door." When it opened the

47

man was standing there barelegged with a jacket thrown over his shoulders, wearing a look of assured indifference. The boy, in his undershirt, sat in bed with the quilt pulled up to his waist. From the doorway Zeberjet asked, "What's wrong? What happened?" "He cheated me," came the answer, in a constricted voice. "How do you mean? Shall we call the police?" The boy, very pale, shook his head. "No. No, don't do that." "I'm sorry if we've upset you," said the other. He turned to the boy. "I'll move to another room if you like." "No, don't." Everyone was silent in front of the door. "Good night," said the man, and shut them out. "Can you beat that," said an elderly fellow. "All right, people, let's get to bed then." Zeberjet turned off the hall light when they had withdrawn. Going upstairs, he undressed again and lay down, but had trouble getting to sleep. Next morning while the man was paying the boy stood aloof. But when his companion said, "Aren't you going to wish the gentleman good morning?" he turned to smile, and in a voice changed from the night before said good morning.

"Good evening to you."

"The same to you."

It was two men, and a sallow-faced woman with her nose bandaged. Zeberjet uttered the formula of condolence that means "Get well soon."

"Thank you. She got a nosebleed early this afternoon, about the time for prayers, and we couldn't make it stop. Brought her to the hospital by train. She's better now."

He wrote down their names and asked while handing them the key. They weren't from there. Except when TEKEL, the state monopoly, was paying for the tobacco crop, no one from the nearby villages had been staying at the hotel much since the *dolmushes* began making their runs. When tobacco time did come round, every room except number 1 would be full. He was about to pick his nose but stopped as though someone were watching.

Hearing the 6:40 he got up from his chair and went around to stand in front of the desk. Yesterday evening she hadn't come. But today was Thursday. "Hello, is my room free? . . ." He ran a hand through his hair. There were so many alternatives, though she would say just one thing. Shaking his head, running a hand through his hair, or telling himself with impatience to let it go never drove all this out of his mind—not only the possible greetings, but the insignificant details connected to it. . . .

The door opened. It was a smartly dressed man. That face. . . .

"Do you have a single?"

"Could I reserve it? I'll be back."

The man turned and left. That dark, spare face, with a hint of mockery to the eyes and mouth. He'd seen it before. So she wouldn't be coming tonight either. Couldn't her brother or whoever tell her to leave (or offer to leave with her) before Republic Day? Maybe they had already brought her one morning by some other means to meet the Ankara-bound train. He shook his head. Pulled the collar of his sweater down a touch. He had bathed that morning and shaved. (The barber's boy had come for him that afternoon. "Tell him I got a haircut the other day." The boy had gone, to be replaced shortly by the barber himself. "Zeberjet Efendi, if we've done something amiss. . . ." "No, no. I was downtown Monday and had my hair cut there." "When the boy told me, I thought you might have left us for good." "No, I'll

49

be in again." "I see you had your mustache removed, too." "I suppose so." "That was a good idea. You look younger." The barber left. "What did he want?" asked the Retired Officer. "For me to get a haircut.") While shaving he'd been careful to slide the razor gently over the nick at the right corner of his mouth. Drying his face, he saw that there was no blood. But he still went through the motions of stanching with the towel. Dressed, he headed downstairs, then turned back part way to the third floor and woke up the maid. On Thursdays she went to the marketplace for the week's vegetables. Toward morning he'd awakened from a dream in which he was coming and coming. His briefs were wet and sticky in front. He'd sat up, and with the dripping held in his hand had gone to the bathroom. Soiling yourself was beyond your control. In his dream it had been strange to lie with the maid, whom he hadn't thought of that way lately. She'd been almost the same as in real life, but she opened her eyes, embraced him, and when he chewed her nipple said, "Haa, I'm yours," or "Ahh, how I'm yours." He touched his pants where it had begun to grow again, pushed it down, rearranged it. Sometimes with a slipper at night in the barracks. . . . The door opened. It was the Retired Officer. For a week now his slacks had been well-pressed. He might be going to a tailor's sometimes during the lunch hour to have it done. That noon Zeberjet had had his own ironed. The man's nose was red, so he must have been drinking again. He sat in the usual armchair.

"It's cool out tonight. How do you heat this place in the winter?"

"There's a kerosene stove for down here. And the head of the stairs has partitioning boards, plus a door."

"How about the other floors?"

"They're not heated."

The other took up his book and opened it. A blessing he wasn't a talker. The Dentist, now. . . . The Dentist would burst if he had to stay alone half an hour. Zeberjet had felt a certain affinity toward the R.O. since the previous night. Just back from eating, the man had stopped for a word. "You've only been out once in the past six days. Do you always sit here?"

"Yes, sir. That's my job."

"Not an easy job. You hold up well." Was his job really a hard one? When Faruk Bey had raised the prices five years ago, and along with them Zeberjet's and the maid's wages, he'd been abashed and looked down at the floor. That was Faruk Bey's second appearance, the first being in 1955 when Rüstem Bey died. In dividing up the legacy the elder sisters had let him have the hotel. "Would you like to look around upstairs?" Faruk Bey was two years old when the family moved away to Izmir, but as a child had been brought here several times by his father. On that one night he had stayed in Room 1, leaving the next morning. The Retired Officer had the book in his left hand, a cigarette in his right. As Zeberjet was about to get up and make some tea the door opened. It was a fairly young man who came over with a glance at the Retired Officer and leaned across the desk.

"Hello," he said softly, "I have a favor to ask."

"Please do."

"I was planning to take the train to Izmir with a lady, but it's three hours behind time. I wonder if we could spend the night here. We're in a spot. And we'd rather not wait at the station."

"Where's the lady?"

"At the station."

"All right, you're welcome to stay."

"Thanks so much."

When he had left, the Retired Officer turned to Zeberjet.

"Who was that?"

"I don't know. He asked if . . . if he could bring someone to the hotel."

"Asked after someone, you say?"

"No, he's bringing someone."

The R.O. had turned pale, perhaps because of the liquor in him. When the door opened, it was the man who had reserved a single. A dark, spare face. . . . Suddenly Zeberjet remembered. Two years ago, this man had left still owing for his one night, and had promised to come back and make it up later. Now he stood at the desk.

"Are you the one who shows me the room?"

"We take payment in advance, sir."

"Why? I'll pay tomorrow when I check out."

"I'm sorry. You owe us for one night."

"What? I owe you?"

"That's right. It was two years ago. You said you'd pay later."

"There's some mistake. I've never been here before."

"I don't think there's any mistake."

"This is ridiculous. I can't stay here if you won't trust me."

"As you wish."

The man laughed. "Funny place," he said, and left. The Retired Officer gathered up his book and newspapers. He seemed to be in pain, his face sallow as he approached the desk. Was he sick? Zeberjet gave him the key with a "Good night, sir."

The man looked him in the eye and suddenly burst out as if swearing.

"You're very strong!"

Zeberjet recoiled in his chair and blanched, and the man turned to walk away. He wanted to call out after him, ask him not to go up yet. But how could he? When the door had closed upstairs the main door opened. It was a young woman with a handbag and the young man who had just been there. They were anxious. As the man approached the desk the woman stopped at a distance, her eyes to the floor. Zeberjet took the key to Room 6 from its hook.

"I'll give you a double bed."

"Just one bed?"

"Yes."

"Don't you have a room with two?"

"Of course, but you'll be more comfortable here."

The man turned to his companion.

"What do you think?"

She shrugged, and said, "I don't know."

"All right, give us the double bed."

Zeberjet handed the key over.

"Third floor, first room on the left. Number six."

He watched them go up the stairs. Wearing flats, she was as tall as he was, with a compact butt and good, straight legs. The man had said they were in a spot. Perhaps both of them were married. Would they embrace the moment they were inside? She'd want the door locked first.

Half an hour after the train from Ankara went through he locked and barred the main door. It was two hours late tonight instead of three. He turned off the lights and went into the room. Tuesday he had oiled the hinges. Last night he'd stayed for only a very short time, turning away decisively as he was about to reach for the towel. Now he walked over to the bedside table. On the bed that night she had been sitting precisely in this spot. Her black sweater, the necklace of large silver balls. . . . And she'd looked up. The teapot, strainer, and tea-glass, the small dish with its five lumps of sugar. He had brought six. Could he know for certain she had drunk one glass with the missing lump? She might even have held it in her mouth to drink three. His hand hesitated. Yet he had to know how she took her tea. Bending down, he lifted the lid of the pot and saw that it was more than half full. She'd drunk a single glass. With the lid back on the pot, he picked her glass up and turned it in the light. A faint smudge at the rim showed where her lips had touched. There was another, smaller smudge that might be her fingerprint. A creaking came from the room overhead. For some time he stood with the glass lifted, his face to the light. A blackened sip of tea remained in the bottom. Closing his eyes he brought the glass down, caught the stagnant odor of stale tea, and where he thought her lips had been he kissed the glass. A sudden crash overhead strained the ceiling and he jumped, dropping the glass on the floor, where it shattered. He stared, his flesh crawling. The Retired Officer must have fallen out of bed. He heard running water above, followed by a creaking that must have been the man lying down again. When his heartbeat returned to normal Zeberjet let go of the bedstead and took a backward step, surveying the bits of glass on the floor. The room had been violated. Now she would not come back. Leaving, he turned off the light, which had been burning for a week.

FRIDAY

It was past seven when he came downstairs. As he was making tea in the pantry, after first unlocking the entrance, a door opened and closed above. Placing the teapot on the lowered flame he came out and sat in his chair, just as the R.O., small leather suitcase in hand, was coming down. He looked tired, washed out, swarthier. And he hadn't shaved.

"Good morning, sir."

"Morning. What do I owe?"

"Seven days, that makes a hundred and five liras."

The man took a handful of bills from his back pocket and counted a hundred and twenty liras out onto the desk. The remainder went into his back pocket, and he picked up the suitcase.

"Keep the change."

He was obviously feeling low. Almost at the door, he halted when Zeberjet called out, "You're running along, then."

The man's shoulders hunched painfully. Then, without turning, he continued on out, closed the door softly behind him, and was gone. Had he realized the woman wasn't coming? "She won't be back, but I still have to wait," Zeberjet had wanted to say. Who knows, the man might have been waiting for someone else. He'd stood up pretty well, all things considered.

After breakfast Zeberjet came with broom and dustpan into the woman's room and switched on the light. He swept up the broken glass to the right of the bed and poured it into the wastebasket, then took a damp rag to the tea stains on the linoleum. Then he went to the pantry with the rag, washed his hands and brought his breakfast teaglass —in which he had left one sip—to her room to substitute for the broken one. Now if she came back there would be nothing to notice. But he, of course, knew. He turned off the light and went out, locking the door. He sat in his chair. The whistle was blowing at the textile mill and he checked the clock. Two minutes to eight. This alarm clock lost two minutes a day. Had he forgotten today to set it after winding it up? He'd check at noon when they shot off the cannon. At two minutes past eight last Friday he had knocked. "That's fine, I'm getting up." Was it only a week ago? He took cigarettes and matches from his lefthand pocket. That he had let her sleep an extra minute or two was not so important, but certain details did matter. Her not carrying an ID, the forgotten towel, the two half-smoked cigarettes. All this meant she was absent-minded, unsure, even if it didn't show. You'd expect a woman going to see her brother for the week to be more at ease. Possibly there was someone else in that village, someone she knew from Ankara.

He was stubbing out his cigarette when the couple from last night came down. The man had been frank. They could easily have passed themselves off as married. She had too much make-up on. He looked pale. "Don't forget," he said, and stopped at the desk. The woman smiled and continued on out.

"Good morning. All right if I wait a while?"

"As you wish, sir."

The man was looking out the door; he shifted, took out a pack of cigarettes, offered it.

"Like to smoke?"

"I just did. Some other time. Were you comfortable last night?"

"The room was perfect. Thanks."

He lit his cigarette and sucked at it.

"We may want to come back again."

"Of course, sir."

The man switched the cigarette to his left hand and drew a fifty-lira bill from his back pocket.

"Goodbye," he said, leaving the bill on the desk.

The man walked away as Zeberjet opened the cash drawer. "Just a minute. Your change. . . ."

But he went out as though he hadn't heard. Zeberjet took the R.O.'s fifteen liras from the drawer and put it, together with the bills he already held, in his back pocket. Had he turned away that deadbeat (was it really the same man?) in order to give this couple Room 6? Going up to bed at night he had stopped to listen at the R.O.'s door, and had been considering a knock when the creak of bedsprings, coupled with a blanket-stifled cough, sent him on up to the third floor. There he had leaned to the dark keyhole of Room 6. The words of a quiet conversation came through the door, indistinguishable. Perhaps they were only resting. There was a creak. "Smoke?" "All right," said the woman. Zeberjet had gone to his room.

NIGHT

Long after the 6:40 had passed through he was pacing between the door and the stairs, hands clasped behind his back. The door opened and a youngish man of medium height appeared.

"We're full up, sir."

"Really? Fair enough."

The man left. Early that evening Zeberjet had told two other people the same thing. The maid had swabbed the lobby floor that afternoon, when the upstairs cleaning was done, and had stood with her pail at the door of Room 1.

"Does this one need swabbing, agha?" "No, it's clean." Was it? He went into the pantry, brewed some tea, and came back to sit in the corner armchair. The large copper ashtray was empty. Was this the final night? The old manor house, after all its years of childbirth, living and dying, was ready now. The train had not brought her; he would wait another hour. Until eleven. The door opened and he saw a blonde prostitute who occasionally spent the night. She was with a middle-aged man. Zeberjet didn't bother to get up.

"There's no room," he said.

"Wha. . . . Why ever not? This is where we've always stayed."

"Let's go," said the man.

"Isn't there anything you can do? The third-floor room. . . ."

"We're full tonight."

The man grasped her arm.

"Let's go."

They left. Wednesday night she'd come with a different man. Room 6 showed Saliha Alakash and Ahmet Alakash. He shut the register and put the same names down for 6 on the day's form. Then he searched for a name to give the man who had been in before these two. In all these years not one Zeberjet had come in. He put down Zeberjet Gezgin for Room 5. There was a sputtering in the pantry and he ran to turn off the flame. The tea had boiled, it would be undrinkable. After washing the pot he came out to sit in the R.O.'s chair. By eleven, four more people had come, two at a time, looking for rooms. He'd sent them away. Now and then a car would speed by outside.

Towards midnight he got up, barred and locked the front door, and turned out the lights. After taking a piss in the second-floor john he went into the room where the woman off the Ankara train had stayed. In the dark he leaned back against the door. 'Do you think I could have some tea?' The tea was spoiled. He switched the light on.

Everything was in order, even the tea-glass. Was it on the wall hook to the left of the bed that she'd hung her thin brown overcoat? Coming in with the tea tray he had seen it on the bed. She may have laid it across the chair later; then her sweater and skirt. . . . He went to stand by the bed. The bed he was born in. Its maroon satin quilt had belonged to the manor house. Did she lie naked under it? Switching on the bedside lamp, he turned the other light off. Now he removed his shoes and socks, put the slippers on, undressed, hung his clothes on the hook, washed his feet. When he had dried them with the hotel towel he climbed into bed and pulled up the quilt. He drew the long pillow to him and embraced it. "I'd have died if you hadn't come," he said aloud. He smelled the pillow and kissed it. His cock was stiff. He felt hot inside and his hands were sweaty. Sitting up he pushed the quilt back. His chest had little hair. His face was off color, strained. From the bedstead he took the towel she had forgotten, with its broad red and yellow stripes and narrow black ones. He spread it in the center of the sheet with one end of the flat pillow underneath, and lying down embraced them. Again he said aloud, "I'd have died if you hadn't come." Apparently she had asked something; he answered yes. His arms were thin and hairy. There were pimples among the hair on his butt. Steadily he rose and fell. Lifting his face from the pillow he said, in a high voice that tried to sound like hers, "Aah, don't let go, don't. Bite my nipples." He slid down somewhat to bite the pillow. He moaned. Legs and back tensed, he rose and fell, faster, more. And stopped. In a high, tired voice, as though it were being murmured in his ear, he said, "Ahh, how I'm yours."

It was the fifth night. He rose to his knees on the bed and bunched up the towel. With a dry spot he wiped the sticky wetness from his genitals and belly, then hung the towel on the foot of the bed. He'd been shaking it clean before getting in, scraping off any clinging flakes with his fingernails. But the yellow stripes, especially in the center, had nevertheless begun to take on a thicker cast. He shoved the pillow back in place and lay down under the quilt. For the past five nights he'd been sleeping in this bed. On Friday night he had brought down his watch, pale green sweater, and shaving kit. The next morning he'd gone to Room 6 for the table, which now stood by the sink. On it was the shaving kit, which he was using every other day. Mornings he would sleep in, and after waking up he would lie there for a while as he used to when his father was alive. No one was at the hotel anyway. Whoever came was sent off; "No room." He'd put all the keys in the drawer. Monday there'd been some difficulty getting rid of the livestock dealers. One of them had muttered in leaving, " . . . whole hotel? Never heard. . . ."

The past four mornings he had not woken the maid. She'd been rising around noon, mostly. "Why aren't they coming, agha?" she asked when she brought down his supper Monday evening. "Don't know. They'll be back." That day she washed a bit of laundry after lunch and hung it in the shed to dry. It had been raining. Today she had come down at one point and stood by the stairs. "Should I go, agha?" "Go? Go where?" "I don't know. The village." "Why?" "There's nothing to do." "Well good. You can rest a little." "Nobody comes." "Go back upstairs. They'll come again soon." She ought to have felt freer, more at ease this way, but clearly the change in routine, after ten years, had disturbed her. He had told her that people would start coming again soon. Did he really mean to take guests in? He didn't think so. Whenever he turned someone away he'd put a name down on a form, transferring these names to the register the following morning. Then, when the newsboy was gone, he would pay the hotel envelope from his own. This morning he had told the newsboy not to deliver the paper any more, no one was reading it, and he had paid the twenty-nine days' bill. It was Republic Day. When he opened the door around nine in the morning there had been automobile horns, and trumpets playing somewhere, an all-schools parade. One important item in the paper: clocks would be set back tonight. He'd forgotten.

He sat up, reached to the bedside table, and set his pocket watch back an hour. It was twenty minutes to twelve. After bringing down his watch, sweater and shaving kit on Friday night he had removed the tea tray. The copper ashtray was still there. At one point he had finished one of her cigarettes, lying back on the bed to smoke it. Was he still waiting? The hardest thing was the vacillation he'd fallen into. How many times had he changed his mind over going out this evening? In the end he had told the maid he'd be downtown and not to open to anybody. Still, he had waited for the train to go through. Then, eating out for the first time in ten years, at a small, simple place near the shopping district, he ordered a single shot of raki. He left without finishing it. There was celebrating in the broad square by the Government Building, with fireworks, music, and dancing. The edge of the square was crowded. Zeberjet had never been able to fathom the people in public places. They seemed different from those who came to the hotel. Two men were arguing because of a remark, or pass, made at some woman. Others were joining in. Zeberjet moved off. On the corner, between a man and a woman who stood outlined against the bars of a bank door, was a young girl, tall and dark and wearing a black sweater. He glanced at her in passing, and she looked away. Farther on he leaned up against a tree and watched them stroll toward the bridge and enter a one-storied house. He came back to the hotel through streets he had never seen before. It was dark.

He turned over on his left side. The bedside lamp cast a shadowy illumination on the painting. For years the woman had been lying there ornately framed. "Would you come awake, girl?" he said softly. Closing his eyes he saw her sit up, stretch, and throw aside the gauzy fabric that covered her as she rose from the fancy couch. She sent the negro girls away, held to the sides of the frame, and leaned out. Her hips and breasts shrank as she grew taller and stepped into the room, walking toward the bed.

He opened his eyes. She was in the painting on the wall.

He re-closed them. It had gotten stiff again and he ran his fingers through the short hairs at the root. "Almost as big as the rest of you." That tall woman, under him so tall. Could I kiss your breasts Sure if you want and your neck too Go ahead sure but his lips barely reached if he was slow ever slow in coming she had a practiced grind an up and down up and down a rocking like the attic cradle rocking. . . .

WEDNESDAY

"We're full up," he said. There was a frog in his throat. He cleared it. "There's no room, sir." This was the first one all day. Face in shadow by the door. Now it would start again, hours of "There's no room" or "We're full." When the man had left Zeberjet got up to turn on the lights, then took the DOOR LOCKED AT MIDNIGHT sign from the wall and brought it to the desk. In bold letters he wrote CLOSED on the back. No need to give a reason, cleaning, repairs or the like. He pinned the card to the doorjamb, then turned to see the maid by the stairs.

"What is it?"

"Should I leave tomorrow?"

"Sure, if you want."

She stood there. Just a few days seemed to have aged her.

"What else have you got to say?"

"I made *kachamak*. Shall I bring it down?"

He hadn't felt like lunch that noon, but had drunk some milk.

"Not right now. I'm going out. Don't open to anyone."

When she had gone upstairs he turned the lights out and stood for a while in the gloom. Would she really leave tomorrow? He went outside and locked the front door, testing it afterwards to make sure. Up the street there was a gathering in front of the bakery. When Zeberjet got there he found a car had smashed into one of the sidewalk trees. He craned his neck but the view was blocked. Someone asked how many people had been in the car.

"Three. They took them away."

"Anyone dead?"

Someone shouldered his way past Zeberjet, who collected himself and headed downtown.

The eatery he'd been to the night before was quiet. He sat at a small table near the door. The waiter (reminding him of a young boy who'd once been to the hotel) took his order of shish kabob, fried eggplant, and wine. At one of the tables to his left a man with a high forehead, round eyes, and a square mustache was talking to a pair of men opposite him. Monday to Monday made eight, Tuesday nine, Wednesday ten. It was ten days today. He fingered his upper lip. The double-chinned, bulbous-nosed customer sitting by the refrigerator had been there the night before. The waiter moved between them in his stained jacket, set down a small bottle of wine with a dish of fried eggplant slices in yogurt, and said something.

"What was that?"

"I said your shish kabob is coming up."

Two tables away a command was barked and the waiter hurried over. There were three of them, the two facing Zeberjet both bushy-browed and black-mustached (though they did not look alike) while the back turned to him wore a tautly stretched black jacket. This man had short hair. Four newcomers—three of them young, the other middle-aged—took seats at the table in front of Zeberjet. When the shish kabob arrived he filled a narrow, flawed glass tumbler with wine. Eating slowly, with long pauses between bites, he would lift the glass now and then for a squinting sip. Whenever the door opened he turned to look. A tall slender fellow, in the act of pulling out the chair across from him to sit, changed his mind and went over to a free table for two on the other side of the door. It was smoky in the place and full of hubbub, a steady mix of laughter and conversation. The talkative, brown-haired youth sitting by the wall reminded him of someone. Their eyes met and Zeberjet dropped his to light a cigarette. He hadn't heard the door open. A policeman and a brown-uniformed night watchman went past him to the group two tables away. Conversation had ceased. The policeman laid a hand on the shoulder of the short-haired man in the black jacket.

"On your feet and let's go to the station."

The black-mustached man by the wall spoke up. "What gives? What's he done?"

"As if you didn't know."

"Know what?"

"That he's on the run, wanted. All right, let's get moving."

The chair scraped as the man—hard-bitten, youthful—stood.

"Who snitched?"

"How would I know? You'll find out soon enough."

As the man edged out he shoved the policeman and watchman into one of the other tables, and amid a crash of bottles and glasses bolted through the door. Recovering their balance the two cops went after him, the watchman blowing his whistle just beside Zeberjet, whose left ear rang with the shrillness. The two with black mustaches had risen to leave. From beside the refrigerator the white-aproned cook shouted after them.

"You didn't pay!"

The second of the two, halfway out the door, barely turned his head to answer.

"Your mother can pay."

While the clamor of talk rose all at once around him Zeberjet sat stiffly erect, the cigarette crushed between two fingers of his left hand. He ground it out in the ashtray. The cook was swearing vehemently. With his right hand Zeberjet drained his glass and poured out the remainder of the bottle. As he was setting it down it struck his plate, but nothing broke. He ate the shish kabob, cold now, and lit another cigarette. The middle-aged man with his back turned said, "They'll get him some day." Kilisli had run off with the Master Sergeant's pistol, government issue. Never heard from again. Short, with a pox scar on his left (or was it right?) cheek. Once during class he had butted the sergeant from Malatya in the stomach. "Get up, you. Not you, him. What's your name?" "Me, sir?" He picked up his glass and, squinting, took a few sips. Slowly he set the glass down. The young fellow by the wall was watching him; he leaned over and said something to his companion, who also turned. Zeberjet looked off. In a picture on the wall Mehmet the Conqueror—Fatih Mehmet—was racing his horse over the sea. The boy had eyes like Fatihli's, but softer. "Come here, you. Fill up this canteen." It was hot. In the other picture there was a plate of summer fruit. "Grapes?" "No." He brought the cigarette to his lips. It was out. He laid it in the ashtray. The wine label read Dark Cluster. In the long, narrow vineyard Ömer had said, "We'd come out here at dawn if you were staying and eat grapes cold off the vine." If he had stayed, for one night. . . . A long-faced man wearing a vest and tie held the back of the opposite chair and asked if it was free.

"We're full up, sir."

He was looking at the vest. How many buttons? Six. The man withdrew. His own had five. Six days ago this morning he had gone up to bathe and change. He'd been letting the maid sleep. Tomorrow she planned to leave, then. A cat brushed against his leg. He trembled. Kicking, his foot hit the other chair and people turned to look. He shifted, reached half way to the partly filled glass. Beyond the left shoulder of the middle-aged man in front of him he could see the face with a square mustache, the eyelids drooping now. The man in the vest was sharing the lefthand table with another customer. They were talking. Suppose he put on his old clothes tomorrow, started letting his mustache grow. He gave his head a shake. There was one slice of eggplant left. Would he go back to the hotel? It was early yet, he could take a walk toward the bridge first. So as not to shout (it was still noisy) he sat until the waiter was nearby, and signaled. The waiter picked up the plates, glass and bottle ("Are you going to drink this?" "No.") along with the fifty-lira bill Zeberjet had taken from his back pocket. As the waiter moved off, the middle-aged man—his back to Zeberjet—rose.

"It's past seven," he said. "Time for me to go."

"The fight again?"

"That's it."

"Stick around. We're doing all right here."

"No, my mind would be on the fight. It's a good one tonight, both birds undefeated. Waiter!"

"Forget that, we'll pay."

The waiter was approaching.

"Well, keep smiling."

They laughed as Zeberjet gathered his change and rose. There was a moment's dizziness, then he recovered and followed the man out. Soon they turned onto a long, feebly lit avenue, its center lined with trees. He followed at a distance. At the end of the avenue was an old Ottoman soup kitchen with an arcade, which now housed five or six shops, of which the last one was open and lit. Outside stood a gathering, through which the man made his way while Zeberject hung back. The sign over the archway read SPUR AND BEAK CAFE. It was a grimy-walled little place with three tables, packed to the windowsills inside. Some of the people outside held glasses of tea. A pair of small black-and-red-feathered gamecocks stood on separate tables, with their long necks and rangy, thick legs. Both were quiet, oblivious to the discussion and debate around them, and of the hands that now and again reached out to smooth their backs. The one in the corner let out a brief, hoarse crow. The other, near the door, stretched its neck to see, gave an equally brief crow, and crapped on the table. People laughed. A happy-faced, rotund man took out a handkerchief and cleaned up the droppings with all the concentration one might bestow on some precious substance. He smoothed the fowl's neck and praised him. Outside someone spoke up.

"He'll lose."

"What makes you think so?"

"Didn't you see him crap?"

"Well sure. But they all crap."

This got a rousing laugh. He laughed too. The discussion indoors had apparently resolved itself, for someone said, "Come on, we're going up." They all climbed the broad, worn flight of stone steps beside the cafe and came out behind the arcade where five or six burning bulbs hung from cords on either side of a level, fair-sized area. There wasn't much of a crowd. A strapping young fellow strode with a short pole, walking the circuit of the pit. "Here they come." Two men appeared, looking somber and pale, each cradling his fowl. Their followers stood pit-side while these two went out to the middle and turned loose their cocks. "Go get him," said one. The other, nearer Zeberjet, said nothing but took up a position close by. A swarthy, thick-browed, hard-bitten face. The two cocks—neck feathers puffed up, heads down and forward—made their approach and joined. A brief cheer went up, and Zeberjet shivered. Against his right arm he felt a warmth, some other arm. From the corner of his eye he saw that it was a brown-haired boy his own height, very young, watching the pit with mouth half open. The two birds, beak, spur and wing, were at each other fiercely. Once down, either one was quickly up again attacking. Most thrusts were with the beak, aiming to seize the opponent's crest. The bird so caught would duck and shake himself, with much effort, free. They seemed like twins, he had no way to tell them apart. One flew up and kicked the other, both feet to the head. There were several cheers. "Go!" "Tear him open!"

"He fought better last week."

"Which one?"

"With the short crest. There's a spot of yellow in his wing."

Now that he mentioned it, one of them did have a deep yellow feather on one wing. And its crest was a little shorter. The man on Zeberjet's left, bespectacled and elderly, asked if this was his first fight. He didn't reply. Pressing his arm against the boy's, he found it hard and warm. The cocks flew up, struck, fell, rallied, attacked again. Their necks were long, their black and red feathers puffed out. But they were slowing down. The one with the yellow feather lashed out in mid-air, missed, and went down. The boy's arm stirred.

"Whistle-shot."

"How's that?"

"The spur just missed. He's tiring."

The eyes were bright, long-lashed. The boy smiled. Zeberjet had a sudden urge to lean over and kiss him, but looked away and removed his arm. The boy edged closer. "At this rate he's going to lose." The cocks were slow now, leaping with effort and recovering less readily. The short-crested one with the yellow feather was farther gone. Blood oozed from his crest. But he kept on fighting doggedly. When he went down twice in a row the pole-carrier approached the tall, black-browed man.

"Why not take him out, abi?"

"Mind your own business. Get back."

The man's eyes were intent on the pit, his face grim, one cheek twitching. The yellow-feathered cock was caught by the crest and struggling mightily, his neck bloody. The other cock's crest was bleeding too. The elderly man with glasses leaned out.

"You're wasting a good bird, Tahsin Bey."

The pole-carrier was busy conferring with the other owner across the pit. Most of the spectators had their eyes on Tahsin Bey. Some were shouting.

"What the hell!"

"It's murder!"

"Get him out of there. Break it up."

"Right. Break it up."

No one set foot in the pit. The fight went on. The short-crested cock couldn't shake free. He fell attempting to leap, got up, staggered. The other bird put all he had left into a double-winged blow that finished him. He lay still, neck and body stretched full length. The owners came to pit center, where the exhausted but still standing cock was gathered up affectionately. The thick-browed losing owner grasped his yellow, red and black bird by the legs and swung it with a thud against the pit floor. Then he let fly with it over toward the arcade. The neck stretched longer as the bird arced across to fall between two of the small domes. Zeberjet closed his eyes and moved so his shoulder no longer touched the boy's. His arm was stiff, his right fist tight in the jacket pocket. He relaxed it and let go of the key that had made his palm sore.

"Are you dizzy, abi?"

He opened his eyes to see the long lashes, slightly tilted nose, and low forehead.

"Some."

He took his hand out of his pocket and started to walk, down the eroded stone steps with the talking, laughing, swearing crowd, then along the tree-lined, feebly lit avenue with the boy beside him. This was the first time Zeberjet had been to a cock-fight, so the boy told him about the week before when the cock who died tonight had won. But the fight they were coming from had been the best ever.

"Why did they want to break it up, abi?"

"Who knows?" He gave it some thought. "Maybe they were afraid of going all the way. Of seeing the end."

He took out his cigarettes. The boy didn't smoke. What was his name? Ekrem. The boy asked too, and Zeberjet lit his cigarette before answering. "Ahmet." How long had Ekrem been here? A year, having come from one of the counties. He worked at a wrought-iron shop in the industrial quarter. Low wages, but he was learning the trade. He lived with his elderly aunt.

"Will you be going home?"

"No, there's a western on at the Palace. Why don't you come along?"

"Your aunt won't worry if you're late?"

"She's used to that. And I have a key."

"Do you always spend the evening alone?"

"No, there's Orhan, a friend at the shop. He got sick this afternoon."

They'd come out onto the noisy, bright main avenue. Lined up on the sidewalk in front of the office building there were nuts to buy, a tray that offered syrup-soaked cakes, another with various sesame sweets, and on the corner a man with a cap to set off his round face selling roast chestnuts. With a small pair of tongs he filled a paper bag for Zeberjet, who held it out to Ekrem as they walked on.

There was hesitation, then a smile, and the boy took a few. His hands were browner than his face, and well formed.

"Wait, let's empty some in your pocket."

He poured out more than half.

"Abi, that's plenty."

They weren't quite roasted through, but he enjoyed them. While they read the posters at the movie theater, surrounded by harsh, ragged singing from crudely mounted loudspeakers, he put the last two chestnuts into his lefthand pocket and crumpled up the bag. They approached the box-office together.

"Wait here."

"But ... Why don't I ...?"

They went up the steps. He did not look at the ticket-taker's face. The theater was quiet. They sat on the aisle halfway down, Zeberjet taking the inside seat. The boy was on his right again. Their arms touched as they settled into place. "This theater is the best," said Ekrem. There was peach fuzz on his upper lip, and where the sideburns would be. His age? Just over sixteen. And his?

"Thirty ... three."

"What do you do for a living?"

"I run a hotel. It was left to me by my grandfather."

Ten years since he had been to a movie. That was another thing responsibility—the hotel—seemed to have made him forget. He used to go now and then as a boy. During his teens, too, and in the army. When his father was alive. Once (not here, this theater was new) the man next to him had given his leg. . . . "Excuse me," said a voice, and they drew their knees up so four people could get by. There was laughter and conversation from the rows farther back. In resting his feet on the rung under the seat in front of him, Zeberjet's knee touched the boy's leg. He let it stay there. Suddenly a bell rang outside. With a tremor he retracted the knee. The bell stopped. The boy's legs in their dark blue pants were well-formed and hard. The lights went off amid talking and the creaking of seats. Credits shifted large and small on the screen, where it was sundown and a hatted rider in black came slowly out of the distance. And nearer. The face ballooned. "He was in a different movie a month ago," said the boy, hunching closer. Zeberjet felt the warmth on his leg and stayed put. The young rider comes to a deserted-looking town, leaves his horse at a blacksmith and goes into a hotel. Dialogue reveals he's back from the war, and has come too late. The bad side has taken over, his brothers have all been killed, his land is gone. Next day the blacksmith tells him it's hopeless single-handed. Having a drink at the bar in a crowded saloon he sees (thanks to the mirror) a hand reach for a holster. He dives, kills. Then comes a large room where the middle-aged banker is spurned by the judge's daughter and assaults her. The girl slips free and runs out. "Strange," murmured Zeberjet. The boy didn't hear. Mouth open, he was watching the screen.

At the intermission Zeberjet retracted his leg. The lights went out again as Ekrem was telling about the film he'd seen a month before. Zeberjet pressed against his arm. Images of actors, horses and wagons came through confusedly; his leg and the boy's rested adjacent. A slight shift and he would feel that warmth again. It was the saloon, with a four-on-one fight. The young man's fist connected with a face, whose owner collapsed sideways across a table that fell apart under him. "Wow," went the boy. Their legs touched. Zeberjet was getting a hard-on. He put his left hand in his pocket to arrange it, trying not to move his right side. With a glance in either direction he removed his hand from the pocket. He imagined himself being circumcised, mentally applied the pincers squeeze. The erection subsided. He had used this trick at night in the barracks too, when Sergeant Refik and Fatihli would come around for after-dark hazing. "Hand me that slipper," Fatihli had said. He tugged at the collar of his sweater with his left hand. The male couples—older man, young man—who often checked in. . . . He relaxed his arm and leg and stood up.

"I'm leaving," he said.

The boy did a double take and grabbed his hand.

"Not yet, abi, please. Let's stay till the end."

Zeberjet sat down again, his hand still in Ekrem's. The boy's palm was hard, his leg warm. In the town, they were laying an ambush for the young hero. The judge's daughter told the blacksmith. Time was running out. Already three gunmen had come in and taken up positions, two by the window, the third upstairs. When the young hero appeared at the head of Main Street the blacksmith ran out waving his arms. A few shots cracked out and he fell while the hero came by at a gallop, lying over his horse to shoot one rifleman in an attic window and a second in the church belfry. There was gunfire everywhere but horse and rider seemed untouchable. "What bull," muttered Zeberjet. He turned to the boy, who was gazing at the screen with neck outstretched and lips parted. Zeberjet closed his eyes. The warmth there, the hand, felt natural now. He pressed with his leg and gave the hand a squeeze. No response came from the boy, who went on watching the film undisturbed, unaware. Zeberjet's palm was sweaty and he let go, pulling his leg away at the same time. He waited for Ekrem to move toward him, but no. Opening his eyes he saw a broad, deserted street where two men slowly approached one another. Suddenly they drew. But the hero fired first, and down went the banker, writhing. In agony, he managed to level his gun, then slumped dead. Clearly this had been the last of the bad ones. Now the town was clean. As folk emerged from the buildings the judge's daughter ran to the young man and embraced him. The lights came up. Zeberjet and Ekrem stood, and moved with the small crowd toward the exit.

"Good movie, huh, abi?"

"Sure was," answered Zeberjet with a smile.

What a lot of lying there was in the world. Spoken, written, conveyed through pictures or silence. It would have been child's play for the town bosses to have that young man killed. But it gave the illusion that something could be accomplished single-handedly, and you went along with it. Outside, the nut stands in front of the office building were still there, and the chestnut man on the corner.

"Where do you live, Ahmet Abi?"

"Near the station. In a twelve-room manor house."

"Honest? Are all the rooms furnished?"

"You could say so."

"How many of you are there?"

"Just myself. And a woman who cooks and cleans up."

They stopped at the crossing. Would he ask the boy over? Carried a key, he'd said. Zeberjet felt his heart pounding. He had the words on the tip of his tongue. "Why not come over for some tea?" "Would you be my guest tonight?" "Tomorrow night. . . ." There were so many ways to put it, so many gestures he could make. He had to choose one. Eyes on the boy's face, he waited for the first move. Those long lashes, the tilted nose and parted lips. Not like the ones who came with a male partner to the hotel. This boy's friendliness and warmth were heartfelt. There was no undercurrent of distrust. Zeberjet said good night and rushed across the street, glancing back when he reached the sidewalk. Still there, the boy smiled. Zeberjet waved and turned to walk on. 'Six paces and I'll look back. If he's still there okay, I'll ask him over. One . . . , five, six, . . . seven, eight, nine, ten.' He stopped and turned his head. The boy was gone. Zeberjet began to hurry. He had the urge. There was a vacant lot and he glanced around. No one in sight. Stepping into the lot he heard a watchman's whistle nearby, but went ahead anyway and pissed at the foot of the wall.

The hotel was dark, but the CLOSED sign behind the glass could be made out by light from the street lamps. His left hand dipped into his pocket. What was . . . ? He'd meant to give those to Ekrem at the intermission and had forgotten. He took out the key to open the door. "I always carry a few horse-chestnuts in my bag," the girl had said. Tall, with dark hands. "Hands dark, heart gentle, says a friend of mine." He locked and barred the door. It was blandly warm inside. He unlocked the room, leaving the lobby lights off, entered, closed the door, and switched on the reading lamp. Sitting on the edge of the bed he removed shoes and socks, then put on the slippers. Cigarettes and matches, taken from his lefthand pocket, went on the bedside table. It was 11:20. He transferred the chestnuts to his righthand pocket, then walked around to the other side of the bed and undressed, leaving his briefs on. After hanging his clothes on the hook he washed his feet and dried them with the hotel towel. He lay down then, first pushing back the quilt. The towel was stretched over the bedstead. That red, yellow and black gamecock had stuck it out to the end. Neck even longer, arcing over. The owner's face grim. Like the wanted man's. "Are you dizzy, abi?" The boy had a soft, deep-chested voice. ". . . and they were set for the hanging but he broke his buddy out. They came riding after them, and when they shot his buddy's horse down at the pass he had to go on alone. They were about to go through with the hanging in a square when a bullet split the rope. He rode into the mob and swung his buddy up behind as. . . ." The lights had gone out, hiding Ekrem's face in darkness. The ceiling bulb had stayed on for a week. This was the thirteenth day. It had been around this time of night that the doorbell rang. The front of her coat open. Then in the room, the swell of her black sweater. . . . Her face was blurred for him now. Dark, with a narrow nose and thin lips. The hair and eyes black, the lashes long. But that could be any of a thousand women. Or men. An ugly old woman, even, an ugly old man. He pressed on his shorts with his right hand, ran it over the fabric. "Hand me that slipper," Fatihli had said. Zeberjet had been awake, peering out from between his eyelashes. The face looked even more attractive by the dim light of the barracks night-lamp. It was the second time Fatihli and Sergeant Refik had come around. He wasn't their only target. They pulled the same stunt on others as well. The sentries knew and would tease you the next morning: "Anyone for the showers?" Fatihli had slowly peeled back the army blanket and, using the slipper, had begun stroking the front of Zeberjet's shorts. It grew quickly toward his navel. At one point Sergeant Refik felt it and choked out, "God, what did he do to deserve this thing?" The slipper strokes came light and rapid. Letting go, Zeberjet gave a kind of delirious moan. "Likes it, doesn't he," Sergeant Refik had said. Sometimes when they took breaks Fatihli would look his way. "Come here and fill my canteen." Or in the barracks, "Go get me some matches." Or coming up with his rifle, "Why don't you clean this one while you're at it." It used to annoy Corporal Halil. "What are you, his servant?" "No, I go along because I feel like it." "What good is it to do favors for this thankless bastard?"

But it wasn't favors. He wanted to be near him, and this was the only way. Word had it Fatihli didn't think much of the local whores and sent for his mistress now and then, from Istanbul, to stay with a certain old woman in town.

He rolled to his left and reached for the cigarettes on the bedside table. The colonialist's concubine slept on in her painting. "She sleeps, she does sleep, but then she's hard-working." He lit up and drew the quilt over him. So she'd be leaving tomorrow. Didn't realize her uncle was dead. Five or six years ago a villager had brought the news. It seemed the uncle had fallen in getting up from the supper table. On Friday evening, the villager had said. They'd put him to bed, where he died toward morning. When the man asked after Zeynep, Zeberjet said she had left him to find work in Izmir. No one from Sindelli—a small mountain village—was likely to stay at the hotel. The pair of men who had come, three years back, he had turned away. Deliberately he flicked the ash from his cigarette. She lay sleeping now beneath that slant ceiling. It was supposed to have been Chief Maid Kadriyé's room, a dried-up woman who used to wear her veil even when only the men of the house were around. As a boy he'd heard his mother telling another woman how Rüstem Bey's wife, Semra Hanim, had been one of Izmir's beauties in her youth. Known to all as the Adjutant's daughter. After retiring one night Rüstem Bey had felt like having some of his wife's strawberry jam. "I'll go up for some," she had said. "No, it doesn't matter." "It does if you want it," and she'd gotten out of bed. Climbing the stairs toward the kitchen, slowly to avoid waking the household, she had heard muffled sounds from that room and quietly come up to listen. "Bite my tits too. The nipples." It was the servant girl's voice, and a moan had followed. "Oo, not so hard. I'll yell." "That's it, yell and I'll bite them clean off." And that had been Chief Maid Kadriyé. All unrepeatable, really. Semra Hanim had completely forgotten about the jam and had gone down, trembling violently as she came into the room (this room). "No time like the present," she'd told her husband, going on to recount what she had heard. As the two were departing the next morning, bundles under their arms, the servant girl had been weeping. "Don't you cry, girl," Kadriyé had said, "we won't starve. I'll be right there beside you."

He stubbed out his cigarette in the ashtray. The night lamp let him see the woman in the painting only dimly. She herself, on long hot days with the negro girls, might well. . . . "You like it, don't you," he said in a choked voice. Sitting up he reached the towel from the foot of the bed, bunched it and flung it at the wall, but it unfurled in midflight and landed by the wainscoting. He went to gather it up, rubbed and shook it, batting off the more stubborn flakes, and stretched it tightly over the bedstead. Then, nail and all, he yanked the painting down. It left a rectangular, pale ivory after-image on the wall. Opening the curtain and window he shoved the painting out into the yard, then re-shut window and curtain. He noted the small door between the window and the other wall, then turned and went back to the bedside. His arm muscles were tense. Did he mean to lie down? This maroon satin quilt might at one time have covered the Adjutant's daughter, side by side with Rüstem Bey. What had that balding, gray-haired, loose-jowled, puffy-lidded figure been like in his youth? Impossible to picture. "As a young man my big brother was like whipcord." So Zeberjet's mother had always said. Her big brother. In fact they were only nine months apart. As his wife's confinement neared and he had to stay away from her, Hashim Bey might well have forced, or seduced, that servant girl. When it turned out she was pregnant they hastily married her off to a poor relative, who possibly had deserted her when he saw the light. Would she really leave? He felt the satin. Had they used to throw the quilt off? Rüstem Bey's brother Faruk, younger by seven years, had taken his own life at the age of nineteen, perhaps out of desperate longing for his sister-in-law. It was three years after Independence. One day toward summer's end, as the grape harvest was nearing and the entire household had gone to their summer home among the vineyards in Azmakaltı, Faruk left for home telling his mother he'd be back in the morning. She waited until noon the following day, then, deathly pale, asked her husband Hashim Bey to have the team harnessed. "He should have been back." Her daughter-in-law offered to come along but she told her no, to stay, that Saïdé could come. Riding in the canopied carriage she spoke once, to say "It's bad with him." As they opened the door he was there in the stairwell, stretched out long at the end of a rope, with his shoes and summer clothes on and his neck snapped. They screamed, and his mother collapsed where she stood. The driver ran, dodging around the table (this very table?), which lay overturned on the stairs, to take the boy in his arms, and flies rose off the tops of his shoes. Soundlessly, her eyes shut, Nebilé Hanim had then lain in bed, seized with fits of trembling for two days, and died.

He shivered. Rubbed his chest, neck, arms. Leaving the room he stood for some time in contemplation of the stairwell. A car passing outside on the empty avenue sent a tremor through the hotel. He shook his head and went up. He opened the maid's door, rubbed his face, reached out and turned the light on. Her head and arms lay uncovered. Generally it had been her feet protruding, the soles black. He went over. Her head was bent to the left with the jugular standing out. He felt under the pillow—still there. He pulled off the quilt and hung it over the bedstead at the foot. Her shift was hiked up, her legs apart. He laid a hand on one leg and slid it up. Warmth. He ran his fingers through the hair, cupped his hand, held it there. She stirred then and he stretched out beside her, undoing the buttons. Her stroked her large, tough breasts, and straightened her head. She had crow's feet, and her forehead was lined. The mouth lay half open—she was breathing regularly—and he reached to kiss it, then slid down and bit one breast.

"Ow. Scat," she mumbled.

"Would you come awake, girl?"

He looked up and saw she was asleep. Removing his shorts he laid them on the quilt. Not in her sleep. Not anymore. He prodded her with his knee, then shook her. The eyes opened briefly and closed again.

"Are you here, agha?"

"You can't leave tomorrow. Your uncle's dead."

"Dead? My mother?"

"Your uncle. Years ago. One of the villagers told me."

"It's a lie."

"No, it's true. He's dead."

When she lay silent he grabbed her by the shoulders and shook.

"Get up, you. Sit up."

He hauled her toward him and she put her hands on the mattress for support to sit up. Her face was impassive, turned to the wall with droopy, half-closed eyes. He shook her again.

"Come on, wake up."

"I am awake, agha."

"Take off your shift."

"But that would. . . ."

"I said take it off."

Alternating sides he managed, with some coopera-
tion, to free the hem from under her. Then he peeled off
the shift and hung it over the foot of the bed. She was looking away and trying to keep her upper half covered with
her left arm. He forced the arm down and laid his face
against her chest. The bed creaked as they fell together. He
ignored a pattering underneath it, and lay kissing her neck
and breasts. He had an erection, but when he pushed, it
softened and refused to go in. He waited a moment, heart
pounding, and tested it. Taking his hand away and pushing
he felt it go soft, shrink. Ice went through him. He got to
his knees and saw that she had her eyes shut. With a lunge
he seized her throat. As she jerked violently and opened
her eyes, he closed his. Her knee rammed his crotch and he
clenched in pain. Something moved in the hardness under
his thumbs. He heard a gurgle. Her body lashing, she clung
to his wrists and he bore down with all he had, face locked,
fingers locked, a roaring in his ears, and the hands went
limp around his wrists and all struggling ceased. He loos-
ened his grip and slid down off the bed, only then looking. Her eyes and mouth were open. Sinking to his knees
on the floor, he let his head rest against the mattress. His
arms ached. He worked his fingers. There was a dryness
in his mouth. The roaring in his ears had abated. Something warm and soft brushed against his leg and his head
snapped up. The cat. He stroked it, full length from head
to tail. The cat, purring and arching its back as he stroked,
put its front paws on his leg, digging and releasing with the
claws. He could feel the living warmth under his hand. He
was getting a hard-on. Shoving the animal away he rose
and went to the door, but after opening it came back to put

on his slippers and get his shorts. Then he turned the cat out, switched off the light, stepped into the hall, and shut the door. He walked quickly downstairs to the room. The reading lamp was on. Draping his shorts over the foot of the bed he spread the towel, pulled the pillow into position under it, and lay down. Panting, groaning, he came long and full. The hotel was silent. When he had dried the wetness off he hung the towel over the bedstead again and pulled it taut, then put his shorts on. As he lay down he arranged the pillow and covered himself with the quilt, leaving his arms exposed. His eyes were focused unblinkingly on the round, white lampshade overhead at the end of its lead pipe. A noise came and he leapt out of bed, intent, unbreathing. Upstairs. He ran up barefoot, slowing on the final flight. The cat was scratching at the door of her room. Seeing him it mewed. It liked having her near, and always spent the day around her, but had never begged this way at night when left in the hall. Sometimes when he was on her a sound under the bed, a furious scratching at the linoleum, had startled him, and he had shut the cat out of the room. He turned on the hall light and the animal mewed. What was he going to do with it? Turn it out, it would jump up at the door and windows, possibly yowl. Corner it in the room. . . . He opened his door and called. The cat meowed. He called again. No luck. With a shake of the head he walked over, opening her door (at the first crack the cat streaked in) to enter. By the hall light, even dimmer here, she looked—yes—asleep, stretched out naked in the middle of the bed. "C'mere." He picked up a shabby slipper and threw it. The cat darted by and crouched in the corner, to the right of the door. Taking up the copper pitcher from the bedside chest Zeberjet advanced. As he raised the pitcher water spilled onto his shoulder and down his front. The cat shot along the base of the wall, over the chest, and jumped to the window. It scratched at the panes and turned in a crouch, mewing sharply. Its body coiled, the eyes on his. Zeberjet advanced. The cat gave a sudden leap that he met in mid-air with arms raised, but at the collision something slashed his forehead. He froze, deathly pale, and swallowed hard. Slowly he set down the pitcher, moving from the chest to the mirror on the wall. A little scratch was all. He wiped away the drop of blood near his eyebrow. No other bleeding. Amazing how this docile, patient animal could suddenly turn. Zeberjet went slowly to the door, and flattened himself. A scampering under the bed and it darted out into the hall. He put out the light and closed the door behind him. The cat was huddled in a corner. In the kitchen Zeberjet took the smallest of three frying pans down and held it behind his back as he reemerged. He called softly and the cat meowed. Down on one knee he smiled, cajoling, "Here puss, here. No one will hurt you," and held out his left hand as though offering a scrap. The cat straightened and came slowly out. It rubbed against his hand. Animals forget so easily. He gripped the handle tight, stroking the cat with his free hand and pushing its head away. He raised the pan, snatched his hand off the cat's neck and struck, immediately jumping to his feet. The cat lay convulsing. Again he struck it on the head. Tail and legs stiffened, there was a rigid trembling, and stillness. One eye stood out of its socket, and blood lay on the linoleum. He set the pan down beside the cat and flexed his fingers. The one before had been a tabby, female. The maid had come to tell him, "The cat's been missing three days. Will it come back?" "Three days? It's dead then. You never find their bodies." So his father had told him. "What's a hotel without a cat?" He had asked the barber for this one.

A tiny thing when he brought it home. Picking it up by the tail he carried it over and opened the window. No one below. He let fly and it landed in the gutter. Cold outside. He shut the window. Then went back to the kitchen with the pan, washed it, hung it up. There was a large pot on the kerosene stove and he leaned to look. *Kachamak*. His legs gave way and he held onto the stone counter, kneeling to lay his head against its coolness. The quaking in his shoulders gradually stilled. Gripping the counter he heaved himself up. "Absurd," he said softly. He turned off the kitchen and hall lights and went downstairs. Going toward the bed he spotted his slippers and bent down, placing them on the linoleum under the sink while he washed his feet again. He lay down then and covered himself with the quilt. His gaze was on the lampshade at the end of the lead pipe that hung from the ceiling. One day he'd had her dust it with a cloth while he held the chair steady on the bed, a large copper pan under each leg to protect the quilt. "The hotel is all yours. Make sure you get a woman in." She had stood tiptoe on the chair with arms raised, her large feet bare and the black-patterned bloomers rolled up. "It's done, agha." Stepping down off the chair she had rested one hand on his shoulder for support. "Trim those nails." This room was swabbed every two weeks even when no one stayed in it. Always ready. Here in the twelve-room manor house. All yours. Where villagers, tobacco farmers in town for the crop payments, Party delegates, dentists, people discharged from the hospital, patients if the hospital was full, newly enlisted soldiers, marketplace vendors, livestock dealers, people with a new job, or looking, teachers, students with an exam to take, lawyers, touring actors, one-night couples, the so-called Retired Officer, the maid, the woman off the delayed. . . . He sat bolt upright. The doorbell was ringing.

So far into the night, who . . . ? Three more short rings. Didn't they see the hotel was CLOSED? He waited. No sound came. Pulling the quilt up he lay back and closed his eyes. Who could it have been? A wanted man? A traveler who had missed connections? Someone who had fought with his wife in bed? A whore who had failed to please? The woman off the delayed train from Ankara? "She can go to hell," he said very quietly.

MONDAY

He sat up. A bell was ringing. The alarm. He reached out to the bedside table and pressed the button to silence it. Seven-thirty—he'd brought in the clock at bedtime and set it, as they might be leaving early. He had slept well, except when the buzzing of a wasp near his face had sent him scrambling out of bed to search the sheets, at 2:10. The couple who had stayed in Room 6 ten days ago, Thursday night, were there again. Below the body, unaware. Young and warm and alive. He had recognized them as they came in last night and for some reason he'd been unable to say no. "Hello, it's us again." The man had looked at him like a friend. Fishing their key from the drawer he had extended it. "No one's stayed in the room since you were here. Have a good night." The woman had turned to smile as they were going up. Zeberjet got out of bed. Before soaping his face he looked in the mirror at the small scratch over his left eyebrow. Only an indistinct redness there. He had picked the scab off the day before.

At breakfast he had three glasses of tea and nibbled at a *simit* with white cheese. He had no appetite any more. Drank lots of tea and, every lunch and dinner, forced down a few bites of bread and cheese. The morning before he had gotten four *simits* from a passing vendor. The bread was all gone. He hadn't been out since that night. Worst of all was keeping the hotel open. The card hung on the wall as usual—DOOR LOCKED AFTER MIDNIGHT. He'd been telling people the rooms were all taken. Toward noon the day before he had gone up to lock the door on the body, hanging the key in the kitchen where the *kachamak* had begun to spoil. This he had dumped in the garbage, which he had then carried down to the shed. He stood up, took the tray into the pantry, and brushed his teeth. Coming back to the desk he reached for his pocket, but stopped. No more cigarettes. He'd get some when he went out. He had to send a money order and then go to the police.

He opened up the two registers on his desk. He no longer invented names for the clients he turned away, but rather had extracted last year's register from the chest underneath the stairs and was copying names from it day for day onto the forms and into the current log. Last year November 3rd had been a Saturday. There had been eight guests. He copied the names for Room 6 with no alteration. There was movement overhead as he closed the register and put the form into the drawer with the others. He had balanced the accounts for October and now began to fill out a postal money order. Upstairs the door opened and closed, and descending footsteps paused momentarily on the second floor. He set down his pen. They were smiling as they appeared, the woman made up, the man wan-looking. They were possibly the last guests who would stay here.

"Good morning to you."

"Good morning."

The man went for his back pocket.

"Never mind. You were my guests last night."

"Oh, but we wouldn't think of. . . ."

"Please. I insist. Do you have a cigarette?"

The man reached out a pack with his left hand and with his right held the flame of a yellow lighter to the tip.

"You're very kind."

He shrank back into the chair and felt the color drain from his face.

"It's not kindness," he said.

"See you soon."

"Soon? But we'll be closed for a while."

"Why is that? What for?"

"Various things. The cleaning and so on should take a month."

"Really? Well, be good to yourself."

"Goodbye," the woman said.

"Goodbye."

The two left together. Obviously they no longer worried about being seen. He finished his cigarette and crushed it out before taking up the pen. When he had filled out the money order he opened the safe and emptied all the cash from the hotel envelope onto the desk. Faruk Bey's share went into his inside pocket along with the postal order, and the maid's wage into her envelope. When the proceeds for the first three days of November had been tucked into the hotel envelope he put the remainder of his month's wages in his back pocket and replaced the envelope. Then he transferred a single lira from the copper bowl on the shelf to the one below. He shut the safe, took a week's worth of forms from the drawer, and put these in his pocket. The clock showed almost nine.

He left the hotel and locked the door. It was a mild, sunny day. The people out on the street had the look of being led someplace unawares. At the post office Zeberjet waited behind a gray-haired man with a hump back, then handed across the money. The clerk gave him a receipt and glanced up.

"Are you related to Faruk Kecheji?"

"We're cousins. His father, my mother."

He left the post office, turned right at the main intersection, and strolled to the police station near the courthouse, which he had passed on his way to send the money order. He pushed open the windowed double doors and encountered the same smell that always awaited him back at the hotel when he'd been out. People came through doorways or sat on benches in the wide corridor. Taking out the forms, he was headed toward a door to the right that stood ajar when a voice on the other side, deep and masculine, stopped him in his tracks. "For the record! To question put, colon, declares husband deserted of his own will." A typewriter clacked. Some woman was crying, and the deep voice came again. "Pipe down, woman, or I'll throw you out." A policeman carrying several sheets of paper approached Zeberjet.

"What is it? What are you standing around for?"

"I brought these in."

"What are they?"

"Check-in forms, from the hotel."

"Ah. In there."

A whole tray of tea-glasses and small coffee-cups, each covered with a saucer, went in through the indicated door, casually swung open by its round, hanging handle in the grip of a white-aproned boy. Zeberjet followed. "What kept you?" "Just letting it steep, abi." The room, full of file-choked glass cabinets, had three desks at which two uniformed men were seated and a third, in civilian clothing, who wore glasses. The boy had set down the required tea and moved on. The man dropped both sugar cubes into his tea and then glanced up over the rim of his glasses.

"Was there something?"

"I've brought the hotel forms."

"Put them there."

Zeberjet laid the forms on a thick log-book at one corner of the cluttered desk. The man, elderly and moon-faced, sat impassively stirring his tea. The hands were brown, with a ring . . .

"That's all. What are you waiting for?"

. . . on the middle finger. He collected his wits.

"I've always sent these in with the newsboy. From now on I'll be bringing them myself."

"That's good to hear."

The policeman at the desk to the left spoke.

"He could mail them in."

During the laughter that followed, the moon face was wreathed in wrinkles. Zeberjet turned and went out of the room and out of the station. It was a mild, sunny day. A bus had just unloaded some passengers in front of the court-house and was slowly getting under way again, as a young-ster hung out the back door shouting "Izmir, Izmir, Izmir," then banged the door shut when the bus picked up speed. The company used to sing while marching, "Ankara, An-kara, lovely Ankara." A smoke. He crossed the street to a grocer's and bought cigarettes, matches, tea, sugar, canned goods, bread, sausage, and cheese.

Upon opening the hotel door and entering, he sniffed. Same smell as always. He emptied his package in the pan-try and arranged the contents. The cigarettes and matches he put in the middle drawer of his desk. As he was headed for the stairs, meaning to straighten up in Room 6, the door opened. There stood two youths, one short, the other of medium build. They were cleanly dressed.

"Hello. Are you the hotel-keeper?"

"I am, but we're all full."

"We don't plan to stay. The bey sent us from the village."

"From the village? What bey?"

His voice was constricted. The youth leered and nudged his shorter companion.

"Hear that? 'What bey?'"

"I heard," said the other.

"What bey do you think? The veterinarian. We've come to get the towel."

Zeberjet's right hand leaned on the desktop.

"Towel? What do you mean?"

"The towel. A woman who came to visit the bey left it here. Two weeks back."

"Woman? Woman?"

"A good-looking woman. She stayed here for one night."

"Oh, I remember. It was a Thursday. Is she in the village now?"

"No, she's left. We brought her to town Friday to catch the train."

"How are she and this bey related?"

The boy leered.

"Hear that? 'How are she and this bey related?'"

"I heard," said the other.

"Never mind how they're related. Just give us the towel."

The towel no longer mattered. But how could he give it to them with all that dried crust?

"I haven't seen any towel."

"It had yellow and red stripes. And black. She described it to the bey."

"Well, I told you I haven't seen it."

The boy stiffened.

"Look here," he said, "she wouldn't lie."

"It's the maid who cleans the rooms. Why don't we go up, though, and have a look."

He picked out the key to Room 2. As they were climbing the boy spoke.

"Make sure you don't try anything."

There was no point, but still he put the key in the lock, turned it, and opened the door. His eyes widened. The towel hung over the foot of the bed. He felt a shove from behind, and one of the boys cursed. Zeberjet picked up the towel. It was a replica of the one in the room below, with broad red and yellow stripes and narrow black ones. The boy yanked it away from him. Zeberjet's legs were shaking and he sat down on the bed. A stack of newspapers lay on the chair. So the Retired Officer, then, had left his towel, too.

" . . . with this liar?"

"Beat him up, maybe."

"No, he might snap."

"We could tie him to the bed."

"Have to have a rope."

They were standing by the window.

"Look, there's a clothesline in the shed."

"Run and get it."

The dark, shorter boy ran out. This other one was fair-haired with regular features. No one but a peasant could have those strong, raw-boned hands, which held the towel, now folded. Whoever this veterinarian bey was would take it for hers. So she had stayed there in the village for two weeks. Friday morning. . . .

"This bey, the veterinarian. Did he come to see her off?"

"How could he? A horse threw him last month. Broke his leg in two places. It's still in a cast."

"His name wouldn't be Ömer?"

"Ömer? Ömer who?"

"Black Mustafa's son."

"Him? He got himself shot last summer. His own brother is supposed to have set him up."

Zeberjet lay down on the bed. The boy stood watching the yard. He waved an arm and said in a clipped voice, "Hurry up about it." He looked over. "Bedtime?"

"I felt dizzy."

"This tying up business scares you."

"That's not it. You can't go through with it anyhow. Someone will come and turn me loose. Naturally they'll have questions. Around evening two gendarmes will come to the village and. . . ."

"What can you tell them? Don't forget about the towel."

"I didn't know it was here."

"Who else was going to know? You run the place."

Meaning he was responsible for whatever happened there.

"True, but I'll have to tell them something. People don't just get tied up."

"You don't know us."

"I'll say the veterinarian sent you. The gendarme will know where to look."

The boy's face clouded, darkening. He scratched his ass. At the sound of footsteps on the stairs he went to the door and called out.

"That you?"

"It's me."

When the clothesline was brought over he took it to toss onto the bed. The towel was in his left hand.

93

"Let's get out of here. This runt's going to land us in trouble."

Zeberjet laughed curtly. "I told you. Are you tying me up?"

The boy cursed and took his companion by the arm.

"Let's go," he said. Then, "You don't *need* to be tied up."

They left the room and he called out after them.

"You're chicken is what. All you peasants are chickens."

They swore, but kept on going. The hotel door slammed shut. Zeberjet coiled up the clothesline that lay spread over his legs in a messy heap, and placed it on the bedside table. He remained lying there, locking his hands under his head. His eyes were fixed on a reflection in the white lampshade overhead. The window that looked out at the mountain. Three of them, including Muhittin the Kurd, had played hooky that May afternoon, climbing up the mountainside to look for sorrel and stolen cherries. A sudden cloudburst sent them scuttling, half-drowned, for the shelter of nearby boulders. They were soaked through. The rain cut them off from everything. And he had cried. "His mother thought she bore a son. . . ." Back down the mountain at Keskidere they'd stood shivering in a shepherd's hut, drying off by a fire he built for them. " . . . brother is supposed to have set him up." Ömer, with his billowing white robe rolled up, hopping from one buffalo back to another across the stream. Zeberjet had thought it might be Ömer she was visiting. The towel those errand boys had taken. . . . Were she and the R.O. related? Their paths had crossed as she left the hotel that morning. "The room that woman had, who just left. . . ." "She hasn't checked out, sir." Too unlikely. Perhaps they'd bought towels at the same store in Ankara. He sat up and got off the bed, straightened his sweater and jacket, smoothed the quilt. He'd have

94

to make the bed upstairs, too. But when he got there, he found the bed in Room 6 already made. He raised the quilt and saw a small wet spot in the middle starting to dry. The pillowcase bore two pale red smears. Someone was knocking on the desk downstairs.

"Anybody here?"

He let go of the quilt and started for the door.

"Coming."

He locked the door, and the one to Room 2 on the second floor. Holding the keys, he turned on the landing to see a policeman by the desk. He slowed.

"Looking for me?" he asked casually.

"You the manager?"

"Yes, that's right."

On the bottom step, in front of Room 1, he stumbled.

"Easy does it," said the policeman. "What were you doing up there?"

"Who, me? Cleaning the rooms." He put the keys down.

"Don't you have a woman for that?"

"Of course, but she's on leave. It's been five days."

"Anyhow, we're looking for someone you may have seen."

"Oh?"

"An all points came from Ankara this morning. Let's see. Approximately fifty years old, medium height, plump, bushy-browed, green eyes. Anyone like that stay here recently?"

He held out a photo. It was the Retired Officer, but the wrinkles in his forehead didn't show.

"He had on a pale green sweater. Came two weeks ago last Friday. He stayed just a week."

"One week?"

"Yes. Here's the name from his ID."

He leafed through the register and came to Friday.

"Mahmut Görgün," said the policeman, bending to see. "That's not his name, but he'll have false papers. Friday, October 18th. There. How did he spend his time?"

"Sat in that armchair, mainly. Reading the papers. A bushel of newspapers every day. He'd come down toward noon and go out for lunch. Ate his suppers out, too."

The policeman was taking notes.

"His name was on the forms."

"Forms?"

"The police forms. I sent them in as usual."

"Oh, those. No one ever looks. They're stashed away someplace."

That was a shock. The forms that he had so painstakingly filled out and faithfully sent in all these years— he and before him his father—were ignored. He had always thought they somehow put him in touch with the higher-ups.

"Why do they want them filled out?"

"There must be a good reason. Enough of this."

And the policeman again held out the photo.

"That's him, you say?"

"Yes, that's the Retired Officer."

"That skunk told you he was an officer?"

"Wasn't he?"

The other laughed.

"When did he check out?"

"Ten days ago. Friday morning."

"How would you describe him? As he was leaving."

"Same clothes as usual. He carried a small leather suitcase. Hadn't shaved that morning. He looked unwell."

The other jotted something down and folded the note into his pocket.

"Fair enough. See you."

"Good day, sir."

As the policeman left Zeberjet called out.

"What's he charged with?"

The other turned with a leer to quip, "Running white slaves to Africa." But he turned around again while opening the door, grim now.

"He knocked off his daughter."

"Knocked up his daughter?"

"Knocked her off. Strangled her. The janitor reported three days ago when the apartment building began to stink."

After the policeman had gone Zeberjet sat down behind his desk, looking at the R.O.'s chair. Strangled her. Nothing should surprise. They had both killed a person in their lives. The first few days Zeberjet had thought the R.O. was waiting for that woman. Hadn't he been? He might have seen her once with his daughter, or found a resemblance. 'On the run. You can't stay on the run forever.' Sitting down here with a book or newspaper as prop. Closer to danger though it might be, it could never match the strain of waiting upstairs, of wondering 'Is this it?' each time he heard a door, or footsteps, or some unidentifiable noise. Down here at least he would know if the door had opened or not.

The door opened. It was the neighborhood grocer who came in, a tall, slender man.

"Hello. Just thought I'd ask after your maid. Is she sick?"

"Maid? Why should . . . ?"

"She hasn't come in shopping for the past few days."

"Oh, of course. She's gone to her village. To her uncle's funeral."

"Is that so!"

"She'll be there a month. I'll drop by if I need anything."

"All right, then. Good day to you."

"Same to you."

The grocer left. Zeberjet was loitering downstairs when the policeman came back, accompanied by another whom he addressed as 'Inspector.' The same questions were asked again in detail. Even though Zeberjet told them the Retired Officer's room had since been occupied, the inspector demanded to see it and they went up. What about that rope? It was a clothesline he had forgotten there on being called down while cleaning the room. The bedside table drawers were empty. The man went through the newspapers one by one. Downstairs again they took a statement—the inspector laughed at his name—which he signed. He felt tired when they had left, and sat down in the corner chair. The inspector had laughed. Did other people really have to be dragged in? Upstairs while they were going through the newspapers his heart had been pounding, his knees watery, and he'd been about to. . . . "Did you take any of these?" the inspector had bellowed. Zeberjet had to swallow first to get a "No, sir" out. Maybe, of all the possibilities, one would, in time, be final. He rose when the noon cannon boomed. The alarm clock, which he had brought along that morning to put back on the safe, was two minutes fast. He set it and went into the pantry, where he selected a can of stuffed cabbage leaves in olive oil. This he placed on the ironing board. He searched around, took up a knife and pestle, and managed to cut through the tin by pounding on the knife-handle.

When he'd eaten he hung the CLOSED sign up and went out. It had warmed up since morning. A young man with a cigarette stood lounging against the wall at the corner of the street that led to the station. Down the other sidewalk came a municipal agent with his leather briefcase. ('Waiting for someone. A girl.') Zeberjet locked the door and started walking. Five years before (or was it six?) one of these agents had picked on his hotel, finding the fresh sheets and scrubbed linoleum "soiled." "You'll be fined for this, fined!" Pink-cheeked and hale, brandishing his briefcase. The Dentist, whom Zeberjet had told, saw to it that. . . . He passed the bakery, glanced at the key in his left hand, and turned back. The young fellow on the corner was gone. Zeberjet went up the three marble steps and turned the handle, pushing and tugging. The door was locked. A woman's voice came from behind him. "Can't you see it says closed?" She was tall and elderly. He smiled, walked away briskly, and put the key in his pocket. He walked past the bakery, the bookstore, the TB wards. Three peasant women were sitting on the courthouse steps, in front of its impos-ing, glass-paned door. He stopped at the corner, where a street connected the long, two-story building to the new jail. The old one . . .

"Shoe-shine, abi?"

A dark boy with wild, curly hair. Zeberjet put his right foot on the box. "No polish," he said.

. . . was on the barrack grounds near the mountain. Part of the old barracks, it had gone in the Fire. Now a school stood there. As a child he'd been there once with Lütfiyé Mola, a wizened, toothless, chattering old woman, step-sister to his supposed grandfather, that hastily pro-cured husband of the servant girl (his grandmother) whom Rüstem Bey had gotten pregnant. Every day without fail Lütfiyé Mola would take lunch to her grandson there in jail, waiting outside the gate. "Who's that with you, grand-ma?" "Our Saïdé's boy."

Knock of brush against box, signal to change shoes. Putting his left foot up he again said, "No polish."

Their house was on the mountain, below the so-called Great Mosque. They would sometimes go there, he and his mother, on *bayram* days and listen to long stories of their ancestors. Perhaps that had been some *bayram* day, too. A pale, thin-mustached youth, his bony, blunt-nailed hands on the bars. He was in for shooting Hasan Efendi's son during some drunken horseplay at a wine-and-women party in a vineyard cabin. An accident, or so he was to claim the rest of his life, but Hasan Efendi—a watch repairman—kept after it and they gave him fifteen years.

"All done, abi."

Zeberjet took his feet off the box and placed a coin in the swarthy, dirty palm. That night if he had invited the boy over, who worked at the wrought-iron shop, if he had asked him along, then maybe. . . . He turned and went up the stone steps and through the glass-paned door. He'd been here once while his father was alive, and then to stand witness during the thief's trial. But that had been a petty case. Above the open double door across from him it said FELONIES. He walked in and unobtrusively took a seat in the last bench on the left, as a few spectators turned to stare.

"Which one?" barked the gray-haired presiding judge from his perch, thick-browed and thin-lipped and flanked by two others, all three in black, red-collared gowns.

"The one on the right, Your Honor. Naïl Bey."

The black-mustached man on the witness stand pointed to one of the three men sitting in the wooden-railed dock. Behind them stood three gendarmes with bayoneted rifles.

"Tell us what he said!"

"He asked me to deliver two loads of sand. We struck a bargain and I delivered the sand. Unloaded it in the rear of the warehouse beside the gate."

"Which warehouse?"

"The Ag Trade."

"Where did you get this sand?"

"From Domuz Deresi. We generally get our sand from that stream bed."

The prosecutor straightened in his chair.

"Let this question be put," he said. "Did witness have prior knowledge that this sand was being used to adulterate cotton seed?"

"Did you hear?"

"I did hear the question, Your Honor. No, I hadn't realized. They told me it was for plaster."

"Whitewash would be more like it."

Laughter in the courtroom. The presiding judge pounded his fist on the bench.

"Your witness."

One of the two lawyers sitting black-robed beside the dock rose.

"Let this question be put. Has witness seen . . ." (he pointed at the center defendant) ". . . that man at any time in the past?"

"No."

The presiding judge gave instructions to the court recorder. Then the name of another witness was shouted. The presiding judge conferred briefly with his two colleagues.

"For the record!" They rose to their feet. ". . . view of . . . absence . . . summons . . . Thursday's session. Take them away!"

Zeberjet quivered. While the gendarmes handcuffed the defendants two spectators left the courtroom, and he followed them out. Sitting on a bench at the end of the wall he lit a cigarette. A neverending crowd of people— ranged on benches, knotted in front of doorways, passing through—filled the long corridor to his left with a brute, echoing murmur that now and again yielded up the name, sharply cried twice, of a plaintiff, defendant, witness or attorney. There was noticeable traffic through the main door. To judge by the sounds in the courtroom, another case was being tried. Obviously prisoners were not brought in through here. There must be a door on the jailhouse side in the rear. His cigarette was only half smoked, and he stayed put. When his two brownish fingertips felt heat he took a final drag and dropped the butt between his legs, crushing it out as he got up, and headed into the chamber. He sat in the same place. The court recorder's voice came rapid and monotonous. ". . . morning the best man's family came to rouse the groom we said it was early yet and sent them back when they came an hour later Fatma Hanim commented they're sleeping like the dead to question put witness deposed that Fatma Hanim was mother of the accused Ahmet Kuruja shortly thereafter Fatma Kuruja went upstairs she screamed I ran up and saw the door open Fatma Kuruja was on her knees screaming the bride lay naked on the bed her face smashed and bloody her hair spread on the pillow her breast was bloody to question put witness deposed that the victim had nothing in her hands to question put witness deposed she did not see the copper pitcher to question put witness deposed that as she knew both families she had spent the night downstairs in order to take the virgin-cloth to the bride's family next morning to question put witness deposed that around midnight she heard a disturbance and muffled cries but ignored them this being the wedding night and declared she had nothing to add prosecution asked for this question what opinion did witness have of accused had accused ever acted strangely to question put witness deposed that accused was a good sort quiet and hardworking back from the fields one evening he had lost his temper because there was no lentil soup another time long ago when the mother of the accused was at her afternoon prayers accused came up behind her with a pop-gun and frightened her nullifying the prayers defense had no questions witness Hasan Belji son of Ahmet by Eminé born thirteen thirty-six was called and was advised that as maternal uncle of accused he could refuse the oath witness took oath to question put witness deposed as follows I was roused toward dawn the night of March third nineteen sixty-three by a knock at the door I went to open and was greatly surprised to find my nephew Ahmet Kuruja why that very evening after prayers we had sent him to his wedding chamber I asked what was wrong he said he'd killed her worn out from the three-and-a-half hour walk to our place my wife asked who's there I told her calm down he didn't have much cash asked could I let him have some he'd need it to get away I said money was no problem but sit down and breathe a spell I urged him to explain why but he wouldn't just that he had crushed her skull with the pitcher I argued this was towards noon that he should turn himself in where can you go I said they'll catch you before two days are out but he refused to listen I said all right but wait for dark he lay down on the cushion and slept I had my son go to the post and the gendarme came to question put witness deposed that accused was the son of his elder sister and that when accused failed the sixth grade he had dropped out to work on his father's farm that witness hunted with accused occasionally winters when accused came to village and that accused was a good shot in the open field but always avoided the duck blind one day accused pounced on and strangled to death a jackal he had wounded witness declared that he had nothing to add prosecution and defense had no questions when asked why he had killed his bride accused again kept silence the bench conferred and in light of the accused Ahmet Kuruja's conduct during the trial requested medical observation to determine legal responsibility continuation of trial was set for November fourth nineteen sixty-three at two p.m."

Zeberjet shifted on the seat. He gave a tug at the collar of his sweater. Throughout this flatly read transcript he had watched the defendant, visible between two gendarmes holding bayonet-tipped rifles. Seen from the left and from behind, his head bowed, he was a wan-faced young man, broad in the shoulders and thick-necked, with something of a hawk nose.

"Prisoner, stand!"

He was of average height.

"When were you discharged from the hospital?"

"Saturday."

"The report isn't here yet. Have you anything to say?"

"No, Your Honor."

"You still refuse to explain your motive?"

The young man's eyes were lowered. His left hand tightly gripped the hem of his jacket.

They cornered you or really you cornered yourself whatever go to your uncle for why not toward the mountain and take a rope along I myself came close to . . .

"The doctor testifies she was a virgin. Her father insists he never let a male, not even a male fly near her. What made you do it?"

Father? Her father's been long dead when they married

104

her off the groom demanded a virgin naked that early dawn
with eyes and mouth open I drew the quilt . . .'

"Tell us, now, or it will go hard with you. Speak out!
Why did you kill her?"

'might even be a relief but not all this police coroner pros-
ecutors lawyers judges as for motive these last five days . . .'

"Did she insult or offend you? Did she strike you?"

'I haven't solved that but why a motive at all they need a
story either insult or a slap silence or obedience something to
fit a little box strange how this judge reminds me of the R.O.
suppose he strangled his daughter or wife . . .'

"For the record!" (At the creaking of seats Zeberjet
rose too. A voice near the door to his right said in a half
whisper, "You don't have to stand.") " . . . report to arrive . . .
further communication . . . next . . . be set for November
twenty-eighth."

As the prisoner was being handcuffed Zeberjet turned
and left the chamber. 'November twenty-eighth then.' The
glass-paned door was open. Outside it was mild and sunny. He went down the steps. A *simit* vendor now stood on
the corner beside the shoeshine boy. Zeberjet passed the
police station but slowed at the main crossing. Ahead to
the right he could see the trees of Ulu Park. He had spent
occasional afternoons there long ago. What time was it?
A teenager paused beside him and, glancing at his wrist,
said "Ten past three." Zeberjet quickened his step. Had he
been thinking out loud? As long as he wished to handle the
problem alone he'd have to be on guard. The avenue was
quiet. If he wore his old clothes, the vest, he could carry his
pocket watch again. Or go downtown on the way back (he
patted his hind pocket) and buy a wristwatch.

He took the north entrance into the park. Red earth
mixed with white gravel formed plots and lanes among the

various shrubs and flowers and the tall pines. On either side of the path out in front of the stunted myrtles stood low green benches placed there years earlier by a bank— but battered and in need of paint now—on one of which sat two teenagers whose conversation broke off when Zeberjet walked by. He passed a man reading a newspaper and chose a bench on the left, just before the packed-dirt open area at the park's center with its stone monument to the Liberation. His body felt relaxed, loose. Unbuttoning his jacket, he straightened the collar of his sweater and leaned back. In the extraordinarily mild, still, mid-autumn air, petals and leaves hung unmoving but filled with life— myrtles, pines, chrysanthemums, roses, lilies, and red-blossomed shrubs he could not name, at their root the decayed bones and flesh and hair and nails of all the dead who had been folded into this soil through uncounted centuries until the Fire. For this had been the cemetery. His mother and father were in the new one on the eastern edge of town, but his grandparents lay here. Hadji Zeynel Agha, Ferhundé Hanim, Malik Agha, Hashim Bey. As a child of four or five he had been brought here by his mother on the eve of Feast of the Sacrifice. "Last year you cried," she had said, so it must have been his second visit. The cemetery had at that time been closed with no new burials since the Fire, so that the tall, moss-covered, turban-crested grave markers leaned into the twining drag of vines, nettles and rank weeds in a strangely tilted jumble beneath those colossal trees; the whole cemetery and its jetsam of boulders girded by a low, cracked stone wall pocked with grass and beginning to crumble, outside of which they had stood—as near as possible to the plots of their dead—among a flock of tearful women while his mother raised her face to the trees, eyes half shut and lips moving in silence as she. . . . The bench rocked a bit, and he half turned to look. An elderly wrinkled man wearing a cap and scarf sat on the edge mumbling. ". . . hardly . . . trace . . . birds." One hand rested on the cane between his legs. With so many benches free why did he have to pick this one?

"Pardon my asking, son, but would you happen to have a cigarette? I've left mine at home."

Zeberjet held out the pack and took one himself, then lit both with one match.

"Thank you. Are you a stranger here?"

"Excuse me?"

"Are you a stranger? It's a weekday is why I ask."

"No, I'm on holiday. Till Sunday."

"Where do you work?"

"At Vital Statistics."

"Excellent. My children have no education. We kept the older boy out so he could carry on with my trade, but I did everything for his younger brother. He simply wouldn't study. Now they both sell roast chickpeas. While you were lighting the cigarette I noticed that wart on your finger. Take it to Hikmet the Cobbler, he'll cure it overnight. Have a sprig of monk's pepper with you when you go. He's in the Cobblers' Bazaar, anyone will point the way. His father Ramazan *Usta* used to cure warts too. Good friend of mine. What's your family?"

He could make something up, say he'd been transferred from Adana. Would this man recognize the name?

"The Kechejis."

"You don't say. I heard they had all moved to Izmir after the Fire. The manor house was supposed to be a hotel now. So you're . . . Faruk Bey . . . pardon my saying this, it was such a shock when they said he had hanged himself. We were in school together. He sat near me in class but we were never friends. He was on poor terms with the rest of the class, too. Used to come to school in a carriage, like Jevdet, Kerim the Perfumer's son. We'd all collect in the yard mornings and wait. I can still see him behind the window of that one-horse coach, and the driver in a fez with gold fringe. When the carriage left he'd come into the yard all bashful, with his head down. Some of the bigger boys would jeer. 'Look at him strut,' 'Fancy-pants,' and so on. He'd stand apart. Sometimes they'd shove or trip him at recess. He never complained to the teacher. Then one day a big kid pushed him from behind. He whirled on that boy and grabbed his neck. It took . . ."

"Grabbed his neck? How do you mean?"

"He whirled and jumped him. They went down and Faruk's hands were around the boy's neck. They had to drag him off."

"Would he have killed him?"

"It's hard to tell. Pardon my asking, but how were you and Faruk Bey related?"

"I'm his nephew. Hashim Bey's second daughter was my mother."

"Girls didn't get much by way of inheritance in those days. I never saw Hashim Bey, but Rüstem Bey—now there was a handsome man. People talked about him and Doctor Stavro's young wife. He'd come to the shop himself on occasion, for special treats. Never liked his chickpeas double roasted. (Zeberjet dropped and mashed out his cigarette. A slender boy and a girl in a brown coat sat down on the opposite bench with their school bags beside them. The boy put his arm around the girl's neck.) He's dead, I believe."

"Excuse me? Who's dead?"

"I said I believe Rüstem Bey is dead."

"Yes, he died in Izmir. His son is a doctor in Istanbul."

"Most of them left after the Fire. Our house burned down too but I stayed. The villagers would bring in cartloads of bread. We took refuge wherever we could—in mosques, khans, public baths, houses that had survived, houses of Greeks who had fled or been killed, vineyard cabins, tents, anywhere. Jerrybuilt shacks went up on the burned-out lots. The shock of the Fire was still with us, but we were alive and well. We had come through. (A woman went by with a squalling, kicking child in her arms. The boy on the bench opposite reached back to pick a yellow chrysanthemum from beside the myrtles. He gave it to the girl.) Our old place had two floors and a good-size yard. We were a large family back then. My parents and grandparents, an aunt, two brothers, and then my two sisters. It was my mother's home. My father's father sold roast chickpeas. Hers was a butcher. Full of terrible jealousy in his youth. He'd be chopping meat on the block and suddenly think of her. 'Back in a minute,' he'd tell his apprentice and out he'd rush, aproned as he was and waving a meat cleaver. He'd burst into the yard chest heaving from the run. One day my grandmother was just coming out of the kitchen with a big pan of food when, boom, the gate flew open and there he was. Startled her so badly she walked into the outhouse and left the pan there. He cried about it afterwards, but swore he couldn't help himself. She said it would scare her to death someday. Later they agreed to a divorce but went on living in the same house together, with their daughters. I remember my grandmother always coming down to meals with her head covered. We children ate at a separate table. (Three students went by laughing, shoving and running. The park keeper shouted in the distance.) My oldest brother loved to eat. When there was a favorite dish or dessert of his and it was running low, he would occasionally—pardon my language—spit in the pan. The rest of us would rear back gagging and yelling, and the grown-ups would scold him from the other table, while he just gobbled away. He always told war stories about going hungry, or how they would steal chickens, sheep and goats. And what they ate. After mobilization he had been sent to Hijaz, which earned him respect later as if he'd been to Mecca, so they called him Sherif the *hadji*—the pilgrim. Pilgrim he may have been, but all the same he took to drink and gambling, if you'll pardon my language. Kept pretty much away from the shop. Not long after the Greeks occupied he was stabbed in the back playing cards. Now my brother Hasan died at Sarikamish in Enver Pasha's charge. We were all three of us married when the call came up. Two years' age difference from brother to brother. I was born in thirteen eight but two soldiers in one family was enough, and then I was kind of scrawny so they left me behind. (The girl on the bench crossed her legs. She was wearing flats.) Ran the store by myself. Every other day you roast a new batch of chickpeas on this big charcoal brazier. Have to stir them steadily in the broad copper pan. Summers it's harder. You've got a cloth there to wipe with, but still the sweat will sometimes drip off the end of your nose—pardon my language—hiss, right in the hot pan. (A young, olive-skinned woman sat down on a bench across the path near the monument. Pulling the hem of her skirt well down, she set a large black purse on her knees. She reminded him of someone, but the hair on this one was black with a reddish cast.) You can't trust it to the apprentice, he's likely to scorch them. My father had been dead for some years, and my mother died not long after they called up Hasan. Both of them are buried here (he pointed to the right with his cane) side by side.

You see those flowers? A little better cared for, don't you think? I tend them myself. The keeper knows me. Rain or shine, I never miss a day. That young fellow there with his girl—now why do you think their bench isn't right opposite ours? See, all the other benches are paired off exactly. So were these. After they made a park here and the benches were brought in, this one we're sitting on was right over my mother and father's grave, with all four legs bolted down. I rushed to the keeper, but he had no say. The bank manager sent me to City Hall. 'We gave them the benches,' he said, 'it's their problem now.' City Hall told me to ask the Bureau of Parks, but the director was out when I got there. The next day I went back. 'No,' he said, 'the benches were put in facing each other. We can't upset the arrangement.' 'Move it five paces over,' I said; 'Pardon my saying so, but wouldn't that be a compromise?' I pleaded with them. Four paces, I said. But he wouldn't budge. (Now he remembered the woman on the bench to the left opposite. She brought men to the hotel now and then. The young boy and girl got up with their satchels and walked off arm in arm toward the east entrance.) I knew a relative of the Mayor's and two days later he went to see about it. They needed a petition. I had it typed and took it in. Next day I was waiting by the door when this old office worker came up, around noon it was, with a scrap of paper. He said it was for the keeper, and we went together. The paper ordered that the fourth bench on the left, counting from the northern entrance toward the Monument to the Liberation, be transferred three meters toward said Monument, all expenses to be defrayed by petitioner. The keeper and I dug out the bolts and fastened the bench down here. (From somewhere overhead a slimy dropping fell on Zeberjet's right leg, spreading. He looked up to see a dove. The old man was very concerned, as if it had been his fault. He apologized and wagged his cane at the bird, and when it had flown away produced a handkerchief. But Zeberjet declined, wiping the stuff off with his own. A well-built, mustached man walked by and sat across from the woman with the reddish black hair.) And your people? Faruk Bey. . . ."

"He's buried here. Did anyone in your family ever hang himself?"

"Oh! No, no one did."

"Or kill someone?"

"No, never."

"I had a relative who strangled his bride on their wedding night."

"Their wedding night? But why?"

"He kept that to himself. At the trial they pressed him hard to explain, but he wouldn't. Maybe there was no motive at all, or many that he himself didn't know. They hanged him."

The old man sneezed. He again produced the handkerchief, blew his nose, settled his scarf. From the mosque at the edge of the park came the wailing call to prayers. He stood up with the aid of his cane.

"That's afternoon prayers. Pardon my going on so, I'm afraid I've bored you. Perhaps we'll be seeing each other. Mornings I generally look in on the shop and then go to the checkers players' cafe. Come and join me sometime. It's on the same street as the post office. You know, where the buggies are parked. Well, good day to you."

"Good day, sir."

The old man walked off slowly toward the north entrance, his back somewhat bent. The lilies, eleven-month roses and chrysanthemums under the myrtles to Zeberjet's right were noticeably lusher, light seeping down on them through the pine branches. When he turned to look at the woman their eyes met. Immediately she turned her head away. Her lips and eyes were made up, and she was watching the east entrance. She might be expecting some man. Or on the lookout. Zeberjet felt weak in his arms and legs. There was still a faint white smudge on the crease of his right pants leg near the knee, which he rubbed and wiped at again. Two laughing schoolgirls went by in black stockings and white collars. The mustached man on the bench to his left watched them recede. The woman's maroon shoes had high heels. Her legs were fleshly. She opened the purse on her knees, rummaged briefly, closed it back up. Whatever she was searching for ('Handkerchief? Gum? Mirror? Watch?') she apparently hadn't found. How could he approach her? What should he say? 'Hello Miss . . . ? Miss? No. Hello, long time no see. Hello, how've you been lately? Hello, nice day isn't it? Hello, is that you? It's a long time since. . . . Good day, where have you been all this time? Hello, recognize me? Good day, recognize me? Say, is that you? Wonderful. Hello, I see you're alone. Good day. . . . No end to this. Have to decide before she leaves, or someone else. . . .'

He rose, straightened his sweater, buttoned his jacket. The woman had turned, and watched him as he came up, her face pale. He stopped near her.

"Hello, recognize me?"

"No, why should I?"

"I run a hotel near the station. You know, every so often you come there . . . with a friend."

"Oh, sure. You've changed a lot."

"It's the mustache. I shaved it off."

"What's with the hotel? I came one night last week and you were closed."

"We've retiled the roof. And the painters will be in." He gulped. "Will you come with me?"

"Not today. I can't."

"Please. You can name. . . ."

"I said not today."

"Why don't you leave the lady alone, buster?"

He stiffened and turned, his heart pounding. The mustached customer had gotten up from his bench and was standing next to him with a glare. The woman's voice rose then, shrill but quiet.

"What's it to you. Mind your own damn business."

It threw him. He groped for words.

"But . . . I thought . . . Wasn't . . . ?"

"You've been giving me a pain for the last half hour anyway. Eyeing me like a. . . ."

"Just a minute now, I only. . . ."

"Two people can talk, right? Now beat it, or I'll get the gendarme over here."

The man turned and walked away.

"Bro-ther. A hero in every camp," her voice was back to normal.

Zeberjet shifted. He flexed his fingers, and coughed.

"Don't sit here. Come with me. To the hotel."

"Not right now. I'm expecting someone and he'll be along any minute. You go ahead. I'll come in half an hour."

"You will? Half an hour?"

"Half an hour. Forty-five minutes at most. Don't stand there now, go."

Back at the hotel he dragged the kerosene stove out from under the stairs and into the room. The building was warm, but in case she wanted they could have the extra heat. Behind the small door to the right of the window was a private bathroom, installed years ago for this room alone. He opened the door and wrinkled his nose. No one had been here since the woman off the Ankara train, so it was she who hadn't flushed. 'Well. The scent that morning, then.' He pissed and tugged the chain, opening the window afterwards to air the room. Did the woman in the park remind him ('the nose, perhaps; the lips') of this one? He took the towel from the foot of the bed and folded it away in the drawer of the bedside table. Since that night he hadn't used it. Last night, with his imagination focused on the couple there in the room below the body, he had sat up once in bed but lay down again without reaching for the towel. He shut the window and curtain, turned on the reading lamp, and went out into the lobby to sit in the corner chair. A car sped by rattling the windows as he lit his cigarette. The ashtray was nearly full. This was where he had sat most of the last five days? Would he start in again? He gave his head a shake, ran a finger along the surface of the table. Dust. Getting up he emptied the ashtray in the wastebasket, then wiped the table. The alarm clock was on the safe and he turned it to face him. On the way back he had neglected to go downtown to a watch shop. The lobby wasn't at all dark yet, but he turned the lights on before going back to his chair. Now and again the footsteps of a pedestrian tapped by outside. There was a dry bitterness in his mouth. He belched. 'With these boiled cabbage fumes. . . .' He swallowed, stubbed out his cigarette. Did she drink? Her voice had that huskiness. Half an hour, or forty-. . . . The clock showed quarter past five. She could easily stand him up. If her date had shown, if they were off someplace, if he wouldn't let her go. Her knees were pudgy. She'd sit on one edge of the bed, the front of her black sweater full. 'Would you like some tea? Shall I fix some tea? Do you think we should have some tea? How about some. . . .' As a car's motor faded he heard footsteps stop at the door. Gripping the chair he made to rise. No one came in. When he ran to the door and looked out a woman in a headscarf was walking up the street to the right, while down the sidewalk came a boy with soft curls, eyes kept firmly forward as he passed. She wouldn't be coming. What did he expect from this woman; from women? "She can go straight to hell," he said aloud.

When he turned the lights off and stepped out it was dark. He followed the tree-lined street that led downtown from the bakery, walking the same square paving-stones that had brought him back Wednesday night after leaving that boy, the wrought-iron apprentice. He stuck his right hand in his pocket. The two chestnuts from that night were still there, cold and hard in his palm when he squeezed. He threw them away. Across the brightly lit avenue, on the sidewalk in front of the office building—the boy had stopped and smiled here, possibly waiting for an invitation—the vendors were lined up again with their nuts, syrupy cakes, and chestnuts. Crossing over and heading for the capped, round-faced, bulldoggish chestnut vendor he hesitated. The man had raised his head to look at him. A neat ring of roasted, split chestnuts lay along the rim of the brazier. A spark flew out. Not that he really wanted any, but maybe if he had them hulled a few would. . . . The vendor hollered.

"Hey, what're you looking at, buddy? Planted there like a jew-yard tombstone. Beat it!"

Someone laughed. Zeberjet turned abruptly and walked off down the sidewalk. ' . . . jew-yard tombstone.' He shook his arms, rubbed his cheeks. 'Was I really stone-still?' It wasn't the figure of speech that mattered, it was the scorn. Such rudeness could prompt a hundred retorts. And what had he done? Left. Chose the easy way out without thinking. Sometimes leaving—running—was pointless though. They'd come after you no matter what. Even in Corporal Halil's village. What would he do with himself there? Hadn't the past five days—today above all—narrowed his choices? He wasn't going to run. He wasn't going to let others pass judgment. But there were still alternatives. Even with that vendor. Now, even. 'You're the jewyard tombstone

    like your father
    like your mother
    your wife
    not my wife this woman
    slime
    slime-bucket
    fig-face
    jelly-faced jew
    you'll lie in the jew-yard
    your widow will dance
    a quiet woman who always slept the stove must have blown up
    kick the brazier, chestnuts all
    spill the fire coals
    pour kerosene in the attic kerosene in her room strike
    he'd come for me
    still people to interfere third-degree prosecutor where were you when it broke out didn't you smell hear but I was in bed
    take him down start choking
    night the flames day smoke for sure someone see fire fire
    sidle up as if to buy sock him
    come up and pop one on the jaw
    come up then chop to the neck

fire fire rush in to find the body
questions grilling jail
stood there the old jailhouse door and behind it pale hands
on the bars Lütfi his name that's right when grandmother died
was Lütfiyé Mola wet-nurse mother stand there *put you with*
other prisoners and cuss his face *they'd ask too what made you*
kill her softly behind him with my knife *or dig a hole* could
stick him in the neck

in the yard no the basement drag her down those stairs
slowly some night by the head but her feet by the feet then her
head bump each step and even if no one saw some village rela-
tive inquire might go police grocer might tell said she'd gone
to her uncle's funeral I see then she must be somewhere else
put hot chestnuts his armpits behind with the knife but if he
whirls

grilling trial to reconvene November twenty-eighth so
November twenty-eighth funny they draw it out what for the
judge seemed to look at me said take them away

toss dirt in his chestnuts *get our sand from Domuz Deresi*
pig-face
jackass
cow-puss
mule-mouth
ape-face
bear
hippo
cockroach
mouse
dog
jackal

pounced on and strangled a jackal won't let the jackals
get my mare his uncle's words you wonder strangled that boy
if no one hard to tell would he flinch or not from going all the

*way hadn't flinched from the final choice not hanged himself be
wrinkled bent cane-propped like that codger in park extremely
handsome at nineteen said my uncle tailors beg to outfit him
white linen suits and in the stairwell flies rose from his not so
much as a male fly near her well three cheers*

when he sees the knife he

*trim those nails my corn I've truly walked today go to
Hikmet the Cobbler*

come up in front
alongside
behind sock his cap off in the coals

*the key? Still there rest have forgotten the manor house
just me left and the dead the park old guy crooked peak of his
cap*

sneak grab his cap off let it fly

*out the attic window landed on pavement the street clean-
er next morning must've thought run over what's his name
doesn't have one let's call him Lampblack isn't that the same
cop as this morning'*

(Suddenly reversing direction he bumped into an arm.
"Pardon," he said.)

*'Pardon my asking are you a stranger no but yes things
elude me do I have friends family to talk some morning should
visit checkers cafe rush aproned down street meat cleaver waving would people laugh or scatter boom through the yard door
and his wife into the outhouse with pan of food the kachamak
spoiling how long will she keep two weeks for R.O.'s daughter
but that was a heated building attic's cooler winter near say
three chopping meat on block think of his wife a saw for bones
should get a hacksaw find one at wrought-iron these chestnuts
for Ekrem*

sneak up and kick him in the spine
slug him in the neck

119

do you saw through the lower neck?

good kick in the shins

start with the feet those blackened soles can't you wash them before bed how many sections from feet to hips two for arms no three blood must be congealed sharp blade to strip the trunk meat off chunks wrapped in paper down to the shed every day few hours interval have water boiling for laundry a cauldron people smell smoke think some food's burning'

He shook his head. He was approaching the office building. Turn down a side street or go apologize sorry friend I had no call to stand there or walk by as if nothing had happened, not look. He went stolidly past the syrup cakes, the nuts, the chestnuts. "You're a nutcase!" shouted the chestnut man. Zeberjet looked. That broad smirk was not for him but for the two nut vendors, who were shoving one another and wisecracking. After the banks and before the square Zeberjet turned right and went into the same eatery he had been to twice the week before. It was almost empty, but there were two short-haired youths at a table on the right near the door. Apparently the broad-nosed, double-chinned customer by the icebox came every night. Zeberjet headed for the table left of the door, where the wearer of the six-button vest had eaten the other night. He sat down facing the street. There were two more men, one wearing glasses, at the table behind him. The waiter came up.

"What can I get you?"

He ordered raki, shish kabob, and fried eggplant.

"We couldn't find eggplants, abi. Our fava bean spread is good. Want to try that?"

"All right."

A voice behind him was praising the potato balls at a stand-up raki joint in Izmir. When the waiter brought him the mashed fava beans with a half bottle of raki Zeberjet asked him what had happened to the fellow Wednesday night, who gave that cop and watchman the slip. Had he been caught?

"Don't know. Haven't heard. What about some cheese and melon?"

"No. Bring me an orange, peeled."

He poured raki into the narrow tumbler and took two sips, trying not to grimace. Would this ease—a little bit—the heaviness that had been growing in his mind and heart? He overheard snatches of the conversation behind him. ". . . first three weeks . . . never stand it . . . passing . . . finally used to . . . on the inside even in dreams." ". . . you wounded?" "No . . . pan out . . . two years to the day." ". . . at least . . ." "Sure, but . . . distrust, suspicion, lying . . . never alone . . . need warmth and sharing sometimes." The waiter came back with his shish kabob and a sliced, peeled orange. This one had greenly gray eyes. And his hands weren't dark-skinned. "Hands dark, heart gentle, says a friend of mine." The tall girl who was seeing the ruins with her father had said over a glass of tea the second night that she missed her bicycle. She called it Düldül. "If I don't watch out she'll be feeding and watering it," the father had said. Hashim Bey's eldest daughter, Meserret Hanim, had a mule named Düldül that caught fire. In the picture on the wall, the long gray horse galloping with the Conqueror Fatih (whenever he stole a glance at Fatihli his head would bow) head down and full-rumped over the waves—could its name be Düldül too? Fatihli's name was Serdar. Preparing himself for that woman's return he had decided to tell her, if she asked, that Serdar was his name. When the boy from the iron shop had asked he lit a cigarette before answering. He could buy some hulled chestnuts after supper and go watch the cockfight. Pouring the last of the raki into his glass he drank half, squinting as the rawness went down. As he set down the glass, the table-top seemed to tilt, and he leaned back in his chair. The conversation behind him came more distinctly. ". . . er's man. When he died, Coy Ibo took over the gambling end. Çakır Hasan used to go there and play, and he lost some poundage almost every time. Then one night he makes a killing. Coy Ibo pays him about a fifth and tells him the rest will come later. Of course Çakır wants it all, says he's planted a field of cash there and now it's his turn. They beat him up and throw him out, but he's stubborn, hassles Ibo about it in the cafe a few times with everybody looking on. Out on the street one night three shots go off behind him." "Behind who?" Çakır. He takes one bullet in the ass and spends the next month lying face down, first in the hospital, then at home. Day after the shooting he gives the prosecutor Ibo's name. Coy claims he couldn't know less but they slap him with eighteen months. Look sharp, boy! We need another small bottle and some *cacık* with crisp cucumbers." "Aren't you overdoing it?" "Come on, what's one bottle?" "Then what happened?" "Then Çakır decides one of them will have to go. He's had a month lying on his belly to think about it. Even considered pulling a job when he's well, to get back on the inside." "Here you are. Care for anything else?" "No thanks. He had eyes just like this boy here." "Don't pour me much. I'm feeling it as is." "Come on." "I always regret it later. That's it, now." "All right. Anyway, there's a fellow villager doing time who gets the word to him on Ibo. Six months go by and he learns they're moving Coy to another jail. Çakır shaves his mustache and goes to the train station that morning with shades on. He just waits. Toward noon Ibo comes in handcuffed with two gendarmes and they stick him in the police room. Pretty soon they're putting him on the train to Afyon. Çakır's packing heat, he moves up through the crowd and empties the barrel into Ibo's back. People scream and scatter around him as he hands the empty gun to one of the gendarmes, who's standing there frozen. Ibo took his time dying. The whole next day Çakır was on pins and needles as news made it to him in prison. 'He's still hanging on. Doctor says he may pull through.' Late that afternoon he breathed easy. Ibo was gone. Çakır figured it would have been his turn otherwise. You can want another man dead so bad. . . ." "Did he hang?" "No, he was still on trial when I got out. The Prosecutor wasn't trying to fry him." "But premeditated murder. . . ." "Premeditated, but there was the earlier shooting." "True." "While I was in, old Arif and this Çakır Hasan. . . ." "Psst." "What's up?" "Keep it low, I think we've got company." Zeberjet bent to his plate again. He ate a few bites of cold meat. The orange tasted sour. Wasn't he about to miss the cockfight? He took a few more sips of raki. Human warmth sometimes. . . .

"Heyyy. Make it count, friend."

A blubber-lipped, pink-cheeked man pulled out the chair across from him and sat down.

"That's about the last of your raki. Let's have some together. Waiter!"

What did one say? Zeberjet got up, and clung to the table, his head spinning.

"Pardon my leaving, I've got to be somewhere."

"That so? I don't like to drink by. . . ."

On his way toward the icebox he dug a bill from his back pocket and handed it to the waiter.

"Never mind the change."

"Thanks. Come back again."

It was cool out. Hugging the wall, he made his way

along the broad sidewalk that went past the banks. He felt his back pocket. The pen-knife was still there. When his foot slipped—an orange peel, or gob of phlegm—the friction of the wall, and one hand on the sidewalk, broke his fall and he straightened. Nobody laughed. Didn't people see him? Coming round the corner he stopped. There was the vendor, turning chestnuts with his tongs. Still attentive to his work he cried out, "Roast like a goose!" Zeberjet trembled slightly, paling. Given courage—or indifference—there was nothing a man couldn't do. He pulled out a ten and crossed the street to the vendor.

"Two liras worth. Not over-plump."

The vendor weighed chestnuts in a small pair of scales.

"Five liras if you'll shuck them."

The other looked up. "Okay," he said. His stubby, grimy-nailed fingers whisked through the chestnuts and transferred the hulled nuts to a paper bag. The rim of his cap was greasy. On his dark green jacket one button, the middle one, dangled loose. A red glow of coals showed under perforations in the metal sheet the chestnuts were roasting on, and a spark shot up through. Again the vendor cried, "Roast like a goose!" and handed him the bag.

"Going to a movie?"

"No," said Zeberjet, extending the crumpled ten in his left hand. He took a chestnut from the bag and popped it in his mouth.

"Bozdağ crop. The best." Handing back five one-lira coins.

"Recognize me?" Zeberjet asked.

"Vaguely. Can't say from where."

Walking downtown he put all the chestnuts in his pocket and threw the crumpled-up bag away. "Idiot," he said softly. After the shops on both sides with their fronts protected by metal shutters he came out where the tree-lined avenue stretched away half-deserted. These chestnuts were roasted better than the other night. A buggy rolled past behind the tired clopping of its horses. At the Spur and Beak Cafe there were lights on but nobody outside. When Zeberjet looked in through the window he saw three young men besides the owner, two of them playing backgammon. "Good evening," he said going in. He chose the table that had been crapped on by the bird before it died, and ordered a cup of half-sweetened coffee. Was he early? The thick wooden table-top with its patches of dark green paint gave no clue as to where the dropping had fallen. One of the backgammon players swore at the dice. "It's not their fault," laughed his opponent. While paying the bald, black-browed cafe owner Zeberjet asked when the fight would be.

"No fight tonight. We stage them Wednesdays and Saturdays."

"I see."

"Don't miss on Wednesday. Tahsin Bey is putting up a new bird. He got it in Denizli the other day."

"What did he pay for it?" asked the third customer, still watching the game.

"At first the other fellow played hard to get. Not for sale, I'll never find the likes of this one again—you know. Finally he gave in. Tahsin Bey says he could have bought a horse for that amount."

"Sounds like Tahsin Bey all over."

"That's right. Win or bust."

Zeberjet got to his feet. With a parting "Good night" he banged his arm against the door, and pain flowed from elbow to fingertips. He'd look for Ekrem at the movies. A tightness had come over his gut in the cafe, a malaise, but no aching. He overtook a leisurely couple strolling arm-in-arm. As he met and passed two teenagers one of them spoke. "Brother, you walk like a bull pisses," and they laughed. He wasn't weaving, was he? With a snap of his head he hurried on.

At the box office the ticket seller told him the show had begun. "With double features we start at seven-thirty." He mounted the stairs, holding to the smooth round metal railing. Inside he shuffled along in the feeble beam of light held by the usher, a young boy, and sat on the aisle, center section. There must have been a meager audience, the row next to him was empty. Muffled voices and the squeak of wooden seats came from behind. Two men on the screen were engaged in a kicking, head-over-heels slugfest. Zeberjet's head swam. He shut his eyes hard.

The tightness and malaise in his stomach, though still not painful, were worse now. Had he really drunk too much? Half a bottle of raki, counting his unfinished glass. A cracking and splitting on the screen drew several cheers from behind. Was his voice among them? Zeberjet twisted, saw blurred faces in the half-dark. A shiver went through him and he hunched down in his seat. On screen, a man and woman stood beside a car kissing. His eyelids felt dry and heavy. "Let me come with you," said the woman. "No, it's too dangerous," replied the man. "But you won't be safe either." "I'll be all right." Zeberjet pressed a hand to his middle and rubbed. His forehead was in a sweat, and a numbness had come over him. Suppose he did spot Ekrem, what could he do about it? Well, tell him he felt sick, suggest they meet tomorrow night. Before eight in front of the movie house. There was a prolonged spate of gunfire followed by silence. A shout—"Wait! Don't jump!"—and the lights came up. He gripped the arms of the seat to rise, glancing then at the faces around and behind him. Some were laughing and talking, others blank or dour. They were all alike, though, and all like him. Realize it or not, they had it in them to do whatever a human being was capable of. His arms began to tremble. Eyes wide he ran for the exit but lurched, catching at a pair of shoulders. "What's the idea? Stinking wino!" The man pushed and Zeberjet sprawled flat in the aisle, where a few chestnuts rolled out onto the wooden floor. He managed to kneel and get the handkerchief out to press against his mouth. The half-dried softness he felt on his chin was bird goop—from that dove in the park. He wouldn't be able to vomit. Put away the handkerchief.

"What's this filthy lush doing here?"

"You reek, man."

"Get him out of here."

He had his hands on the floor to rise when someone hauled him up by one arm. The usher. "Come on, move it." Zeberjet leaned against him, his feet dragging, and they made their way through the rowdy, laughing crowd and out. Going down the stairs he stumbled.

"Easy now, hang on. What did you want to drink so much for?"

"Stomach. . . ."

"Does it ache?"

"Tight as a drum."

When they reached street level he let go of the boy's arm and leaned on the wall.

"Should I call a cab? Have you got the money?"

"Right. Yes."

Two buggies stood in the side street. The boy called the one in front.

"Halil abi! Bring it over."

With the outdoor cool his dizziness seemed to be subsiding. The buggy pulled alongside the curb and he staggered to it, climbing up with the boy's help.

"Where to?"

"Altılambalı. Motherland Hotel."

"That'll cost you ten liras."

"Have a heart, Halil abi," said the boy.

"The customer is king! You stay out of it."

Zeberjet got out two tens and gave one to the driver. The other he handed to the boy. "Sorry about all this," he said.

"No thanks necessary, abi."

Zeberjet let the bill fall on the pavement as the cab started to roll. He reclined and pressed both hands to his stomach, a hum in his ears. Why were they going so slow? The driver's evenly spaced, soft clucks of encouragement, with accompanying snaps of the whip, had no effect on the horses' peaceful trotting. Zeberjet leaned forward, hands on the seat, and moaned quietly.

"The lights are all off," said the driver as Zeberjet stepped down. He half-crawled up the three marble steps and dug the key out from under the chestnuts and pack of cigarettes. His hand shook unlocking the door, and once inside it was an effort to drop the bar in place. As he made his way toward the room the dark lobby rocked, once left, once right. He spread his arms and slid down the wall to his knees. Now he was able to crawl to the room, haul himself up, and collapse onto the bed.

(Standing one on each side the two young towel-seeking villagers tie him down, tossing the end of the line back and forth to each other and cinching it 'defile the towel will you' says the fair one climbing up to sit on his stomach yelling as he bounces on him ass bouncing on him

I'll call the gendarme
hear that he'll call the gendarme
I heard
go ahead call them
bouncing on his stomach with a leer the boy begins undressing off with jacket shirt pants shorts naked he's Fatihli the door pops open in walks the R.O. in uniform and shouting what's the idea Fatihli leaps down to stand at attention
Sir!
disgraceful this who are you
Serdar son of Ahmet sir
Corporal Halil take him away the brig five days on bread and water
yes sir right away sir
as Corporal Halil shoves Fatihli out the R.O. comes to sit on Zeberjet's stomach you're very strong he says
I'm spent
won't hear of it tell me how she's doing
I just don't know how's yours doing
she was so attached to me but lately insists on seeing her village
somewhere in Africa?
I think so
you're awfully heavy please get off my
you and I have to run are you
no I can't run I'm held here the dead the manor house
with the R.O. gone he strains to snap the cord that binds him the cat dives at his face buzzing like a wasp)

He sat bolt upright, covering his face with both hands. Getting off the bed, using its edge to guide him in the dark, he worked his way to the sink. He retched, but nothing would come. With his left middle finger he poked the back of his soft palate. This brought a certain nausea so he repeated the step, and retching violently threw up. His stomach felt better. After washing his face and hands he sat down on the bed to undress. Feet unwashed, he crawled shakily under the quilt.

(At FELONIES two gendarmes with bayonets at the ready flank him as he walks through the wide-open door an old man at the entrance [his daughter is in there says a voice] sits sorting files the females pass the males are turned away chief of three magistrates the Retired Officer smiles as his manacles are removed and outside the wooden dock in the Attorney's chair the Dentist says A-OK as four identically dressed black-mustached peasants rise come shake his hand to give their blessing then the Judge roars take your seats today we hear the defense Attorney stands extracting papers from his satchel and reads out honored gentlemen of the bench consider a scrap of fire which seen in endless space one light-day off is like a spark shot up from chestnut-roasting coals some downtown corner slowly round the spark turns this pile of dirt squirming with aimless motion its creatures sure that kill or killed or safe still asking questions they die the judge pounds you have built your case it seems as to the right to kill here such discussion is banned each act must fit a legal slot the Attorney rummages new sheaf stuffing the first back reads honored gentlemen of the bench when on Wednesday night October thirtieth the accused in whose defense I plead given that he has submitted himself to your judgments and who I remind you is first and foremost a male did enter the room of said heavily slumberous woman as he has almost nightly now for ten whole years barring the lapse of two weeks and having undressed her partly-sleeping form did proceed with normal intent to pardon my language mount her the Judge raises a hand your defense I see concerns the woman's demise that is correct your honor but says the Presiding Retired Officer it's the cat not the woman he's on trial for and winks back goes the Attorney's sheaf of papers he pulls out one more beginning it is of benefit to weigh all choices each alternative beforehand stop cries a voice from the rear it's his uncle tall and slim in white linen his mother and father there too you don't belong here cries his uncle commotion sweeps the courtroom out with him shouts the Prosecutor as gendarmes and spectators and the men at the entrance start milling about a near riot and the Judge's voice rings clear be set for November Twenty-eighth)

SUNDAY MORNING

Feverish in face and body, dream- and nightmare-ridden, twitching sharply each time the cat—distant—darted with blurry wasp-drone at his face; fasting, spent, while his feet and head expanded and on occasional trips to the john he would gulp down volumes of water, he lay in bed for a great stretch of time which he realized had been just two days (slowly putting on his clothes the morning after a dream—again a dream—had woken him in the night and, easier now, he had quietly said "All right then, November twenty-eighth"; going to the mirror where he shaved by repeated efforts of will what he thought to be a five-days' growth, then pocketing his watch—it had stopped at twelve past nine while the alarm on the safe showed eight of twelve—he had stepped out under a cool, rain-soaked sky and went to the news-stand at the station) when he bought a paper dated November 7. When certain details (such as November 28th) took on significance, or if finality were sought (as when he submitted his mustache, which each time he looked through the course of an entire day the mirror had shown to be still there, to an expert), then the corroboration and witness of others were required. The large station clock had read seventeen past eleven. Setting and winding his watch, he had gone to a nearby restaurant for a meal. ". . . and I'm neither dead nor alive." It was a snatch of the loud, generally garbled song a deep male voice was singing one door away on a cafe radio. He finished his rice and got up to pay. The cook, handing back his change, asked, "Been in the hospital?"

To return he took the street behind the station, coming suddenly upon the tin arrow—nailed to the corner pine tree by or by order of his father—which, as it was years since any business had taken him further down this street than the barber shop, he had forgotten. Some paint had worn off the arrow and it hung loose, pointing toward the ground. High up out of reach, though. He turned away and walked on, down the lefthand sidewalk to avoid the barber's seeing him, to the hotel and then to bed.

He lay in bed now, newly awake. Rain was falling in the dark. He had slept more easily since choosing among alternatives. Since deciding. The weight he had carried the week before was gone, it no longer pressed on his heart and skull the moment he woke up. Not that the thought didn't occur to him, when the heavy passing of some vehicle shook the manor house and made him think of the two outbreaks of fire, and the Fire, and the numerous earthquakes which this old building had seen, that someday it might finally cave in and then they would find the body. Of course there would be a little time, even if he survived the collapse, to see that no one got him. He felt embarrassed, ashamed actually, before all those people who thought of themselves

132

as innocent, who failed to realize that only crime—some kind of crime—could keep you alive on earth. For two days he had been walking to noon meals with his head down, avoiding eye contact with the cook when he paid. In the evening he would brew tea in the pantry, before dark so that no light could attract a visitor, and have bread, sausage and cheese there before undressing early and getting to bed. He spent most of the day in bed, too. Yesterday he had ignored the bell when it rang shortly after noon. Going to the lobby before supper he had found a notice under the door. They regretted to inform him that unless payment was made by the end of the month his water and power would be cut off. The button outside was connected to two bells, one of them in the attic. These wires he tore out, and went upstairs to stand in front of her room. He sniffed the air. Nothing. Going down he stopped on the third-floor landing to open one window. Clouds were gathering on the mountain. As a boy he used to come to the window toward evening during the month of Ramadan, watching for the cannon-flash that signaled the end of a day's fasting. The table would be already laid upstairs, and at the tiny wink of light from the mountainside he would shout "Wham!" four or five seconds before the actual report, and race up the brief flight of steps to find his mother and father spitting out pits (hers a date, his an olive) into their hands. "Thanks to my boy," his mother would say, "we break the fast before anybody." She never ate olives. Even the day after the Fire, gnawed by emptiness because what food they had secured in fleeing went to hungry children along the way, she had turned down the olives given them by a friend of Rüstem Bey's. What she had eaten—but only with insistent prodding—was some of the *börek*, which was Semra Hanım's privilege because she was nursing her ten-month-old baby.

One of the horses led up the mountain by the coachman had carried two heavy wool rugs along with woolen blankets and a saddlebag holding their provisions and their gold, bracelets, earrings and pearls. Semra Hanim rode the other horse, with her six-year-old daughter behind and her son, the baby, on her lap. She could ride like a man, having learned as a child from her father on a ranch—her grandfather's—in the Torbali country. Two days, and then during Liberation—to keep looters away from the manor house Rüstem Bey and the coachman had ridden down on horseback, the others making the long descent to the smoking town on foot—the boy had been in his mother's arms, howling if anyone tried to take him. Faruk. They had named three sons after the brother who hanged himself. At four months the first Faruk had died, at two and a half months the second. The third had lived.

Rolling to his right, he listened as the sound of water in the drainpipe and running off the shed and stable roof tiles steadily slackened. A small weak triangle of light shone on the curtain in the upper righthand corner. It could be a far-off street lamp, or someone tending an invalid. He rested his arms on the quilt. The room was reasonably warm. He'd had the stove going for a while before turning in. Getting up on one elbow in the dark he reached for a cigarette and match from the bedside table. He lit the cigarette and held the match-flame to his watch. Five twenty. Putting the copper ashtray on the quilt he lay back down. "And I'm neither dead nor alive." Eighteen days to go. His grandfather (Hashim Bey) had held out for five days after they locked him in that third-story room. "Such a great big man, and he dwindled away. There wasn't a sound or whisper to be heard from him. It was me that emptied his pot and took meals in. He barely touched the food. Staring up at the ceiling as if he didn't hear me. That morning I went in and his pot was empty. He asked who I was. 'Saïdé, uncle.' 'Call Nureddin.' 'Nureddin's been dead for years, uncle. Why don't I call my other brother Rüstem?' He looked away and said, 'My birds should go to Blond Ali.' The quilt had slid from the bed and I settled it back on him. His arms shook, his head tossed, the eyes were bulging. When I ran out in the hall and screamed Rüstem came tearing upstairs and through the door. He sank down with his face buried in the quilt." The Blond Ali of Hashim Bey's last words was unknown to them. They made inquiries all around but no one could help. Perhaps it was some boyhood friend, a fellow breeder of pigeons. Nureddin, son by his first wife, Hafsa Hanim, had been the eldest child.

He stubbed out his cigarette and put the ashtray back. The rain had stopped. That faint triangle of light was still on the curtain. "Wake up the light," his father used to say. He could never stand the dark. Not much of a talker on the subject of family. Perhaps he cringed from the memory of their sudden death by earthquake. Zeberjet's mother, on the other hand, would always bring the conversation round to her ancestors, relating at great length what she had seen or heard tell of. By her account Hafsa Hanim was one of the Mevlevi line, sister to Abdulkerim Çelebi, who in those years was the elder of the town's Mevlevi Lodge. She had been only twenty-eight years old, mother of two, at the time she surprised her husband with a servant girl and moved into a third-floor room overlooking the street. The family had panicked. Her in-laws (her brother's wife; Hashim Bey's sister) came pleading, and Hashim Bey's mother tried to reason with her. "He's a man, after all. If you only knew what I've had to put up with." But she was unbending. "I couldn't look him in the face. I'd be ashamed to. He can remarry." The gossip had spread. Some claimed she had divorced him, in a time when law and custom gave men alone the right to dissolve a marriage. For several days Hashim Bey even forgot about his birds. Then one night he went up and knocked, calling for her to let him in. When there was no response he put his weight to the door and broke it open. There were the children in bed crying and Hafsa Hanim at the window with the lattice raised. "One step and I jump," is all she said. Hashim Bey had turned and left, never going to that floor again. Hafsa Hanim had stayed on at the manor house, not wanting to raise her children fatherless, and settled permanently on the third floor. She would cover her head whenever necessity brought her down. Hashim Bey took a second wife the next year and the two women got along famously. She called Nebilé Hanim "daughter," though only ten years her senior. "My first memories are of Aunt Hafsa. You know my mother's lying-in ended with her death, and I needed a wet-nurse. Aunt Nebilé was suckling brother Rüstem but that was all the milk she had, so they sent for Aunt Lütfiyé, who had a three-month-old baby daughter. Aunt Hafsa took me in upstairs. She rocked my cradle and changed me and looked after me when I was sick. Even her own daughter wasn't trusted to hold me, though she was eight years old, big sister Meserret. A carefree tomboy if ever there was one. She'd come at night to rub our faces with soot, plant needles in the wicker chairs, dump water out the attic window on people below, and slide down the banisters. There were finally six children in the household, all sizes. Brother Nureddin, the eldest, kept aloof, usually in his room reading. We always wanted Auntie around, she told such good stories. Bright peace be upon them, both my two aunts treated me like their own child. Presents or clothes, I always got what the other girls did. As she combed my hair in the mornings Aunt Hafsa used to kiss the nape of my neck and say what beautiful hair I had, her little orphan girl. But when sister Meserret ran off with the caretaker's son Auntie gave up. In the space of a few days her face became drawn and wrinkled. She always wore a scarf. Sometimes I'd massage her neck and temples for her. She ate opium and her speech started to ramble. Toward the end the same woman who had once smeared pepper on her daughter's lips for bad language—Meserret had fallen and said, 'Ouch, my butt'—took to babbling out all that she and her husband used to do in bed. Unrepeatable stories." Hashim Bey had dismissed the caretaker and disowned Meserret but Nebilé Hanim begged and pleaded—even though it was only her step-daughter—and got them a dowry plus four acres of vineyard. They set up housekeeping in a small dwelling near Azmakaltı. There had been no children. Years later her husband was net-fishing in the river when his foot got tangled in some willow roots and he drowned. Though invited back to the manor house Meserret Hanim had declined. She looked after the vineyard herself, riding out donkey-back on summer days while she smoked a hand-rolled cigarette. She used to laugh telling how men would greet her in the fields thinking she was one of them. It was late one summer afternoon coming home atop Düldül with dry grass in the saddlebags, a loose spark from her cigarette must have got in. The grass caught, and as she tried to bat the flames out barehanded they spread to her clothing. That's when she jumped, running on fire behind the donkey until she fell. Two men winnowing wheat not far off rushed up, but by the time they put her out she was charred all over. She died that night.

The bed trembled. This was the second time since he

woke up that a vehicle had gone by. He turned his head to look at the curtain. No triangle. It was dark out, the street lamps wouldn't be off yet. Perhaps the patient had fallen asleep. Or died. 'And I'm neither dead nor alive.' Eighteen days. With eighteen days left great-uncle Nureddin had come out from his stone cell in the Halveti monastery. "My forty days are up," he had said. Hair and beard, cut at the beginning of his novitiate seclusion, had grown back. His face was waxen and the shirt drooped on his emaciated body. Twice a day he would leave the cell, head bowed, to visit the outhouse, and coming back take a hunk of bread and a few olives from the tray by his door. The Shaykh had told him, "We make it twenty-two days, my son." "You're wrong. It's been forty." When the other dervishes laughed the Shaykh lifted a hand. "That's true. We may have miscounted." Nureddin had swayed then and crumpled in a heap. After laying him in one of the chambers they sent for his father. The doctor Hashim Bey brought along diagnosed simple exhaustion and promised a quick recovery. At one point Nureddin opened his eyes to smile. "Everything's so right, Father." He died the next morning. Twenty-eight years of age. That old fellow in the park was mistaken. The rumor about Doctor Stavro's wife involved Nureddin, not Rüstem Bey. The boy never told anyone, but word had it that they used to meet in the house of a peddler woman, a door-to-door seller of underclothes and linens. When Stavro's wife died (poisoned, so it was thought, by her husband) it may have been Nureddin's abrupt entry into monastic life that prompted the rumors. Or merely the peddler woman's sly boast of "They knew the house." The uncle, Abdulkerim Çelebi, had offered to make him a scribe at the Lodge, but Nureddin preferred to join those novitiates who saw to the general chores. Two of them, whichever two, but they had to be beardless, were assigned to sweep up the Abdulkerim Çelebi's room, to make his bed, bring his meals, and pour the water for his ablutions. But Nureddin never did quite fit in at the Lodge, and before two months were out he had left to seek out the Halveti Shaykh Ismaïl Dede, caring little about his uncle's disappointment or the charge of apostate that some leveled against him. "They're all soft and lazy," he had said, after kissing the Shaykh's hand. "All they do is eat, drink, and talk the time away." That very noon, following a brief ritual, he had withdrawn into the stone cell to begin forty days of solitude.

Zeberjet ran both hands over his chest, belly, and legs. Wasn't it a kind of suicide, overtaxing the body? In that cold cell, with a straw mat to sit and sleep on and a hair blanket for warmth, unwashed, eating nothing but some bread and olives. . . . Twenty-two days had been his limit, then. He rubbed his neck. November twenty-eighth would make forty days. Last of the Kechejis. You couldn't count the one in Istanbul who had forgotten the house he was born in. Five years back he had been down on business—selling off two shops that had been in the family for generations—and had not even bothered to have a look upstairs. This manor house and the dead, that was the Kechejis now. They had settled here hundreds of years ago. Kecheji-Zadé Mehmet Agha—Agha by virtue of captaining the Janissaries—who served under Mehmet the Hunter Sultan in the mid-1600s, had a son who distinguished himself in the suppression of an Istanbul uprising and as a reward was deeded the lands pertaining to two villages. Included were several hundred acres of scrub interspersed with monk's pepper, and it was this tract of land, divided by a river and until then used only as a sheep pasture, which Hadji Zeynel Agha at the beginning of the previous century, using coercion and the promise of share-cropping rights, had induced the peasants to plow for him, reclaiming thereby a rich soil whose income—combined with that from the other farms—was later to provide for the buying and building of several shops in town. Zeynel Agha's son Malik Agha had built this manor house. It was said of the Kechejis at that time that they could get by for years just by selling the doors of their home and their many shops. Malik Agha held a firm whip hand over the croppers and foremen. Until the day a stroke rendered him bedridden he would be out in the fields on his horse at planting and harvest time, and usually back home an hour or two after sunset. He died, aged sixty-five, when his son was thirty and his daughter-in-law pregnant with Nureddin.

Hashim Bey had let the farmland take care of itself. The foremen grew wealthy on what they filched from the cotton, grain, grape and olive crops. Along with this negligence went a certain magnanimity; Hashim Bey gave no thought to expense. At the foot of the mountain on the stream-bank not far from where the old manor house had burned down in the Fire stood tall warehouses, and there in the eaves lived Hashim Bey's pigeons. Hundreds of every species. A man had even been hired to tend and feed them. There were some pairs he had paid nine or ten gold pieces for, the price of a matched pair of carriage horses. On occasion as he watched them cross in somersault flight through the air, a high-circling hawk would swoop down and pluck one off. This moved him to offer a standing reward of two gold pieces for every dead hawk or falcon brought in. Then the outlay for weddings, holidays, Ramadan evenings and the festivities attendant on circumcision; dowries when a daughter or servant girl married; the saddle and carriage horses, the grooms. "Brother Rüstem got married two and a half months after the *Hürriyet* was proclaimed. The feasting and drinking! For three days cauldrons of food stood bubbling in rows under the shed. And what a procession when we rode to Izmir for the bride. Five drum and five *zurna* players, twanging strings, dancing girls and dancing men dressed as girls. And a bridal coach inlaid with mother-of-pearl, drawn by four grays." After the wedding they had sold ten shops. Rüstem Bey, it seemed, took after his father. The shops that had burned in the Fire were never rebuilt, the land was sold off piecemeal. In the 1930s, when wheat fell to one qurush and the seedless raisins (which had fallen to three) lay waiting in flattened sacks, piled high while the rats gnawed through them and made nests and the price never budged; when moths got the barley, and Rüstem Bey—coming out from Izmir every month for the hotel proceeds—claimed this was about all their household ran on; during those years he disposed of land for a song, and what few vineyards and fields did remain were later sold off, at his death in 1955, by the three married daughters in Izmir, leaving two shops and this hotel as Faruk Bey's share: who, down from Istanbul five years ago for the sale of his two shops, had promised not to give up the hotel, laughing, "It keeps me in cigarettes." That night he had slept on this bed in this room, where both of them had been born. His mother was living with him at the time in Istanbul. Perhaps she was alive even now. She'd be seventy-five. "I can't go on in this old ruin," she had said after the Fire. "We have another house in the city. There's my son's education to think of, and the girls' upbringing." They had moved to Izmir where her father the Adjutant had bequeathed a house in Kokaryalı. It was in the house next door—where Hashim Bey's youngest daughter Ferhundé had gone as a bride one year before the founding of the Republic—that Rüstem Bey long ago saw the girl his sister had praised so highly and who was to be his wife. A dark, striking girl, quite tall, bosomy, with black hair and eyes, long lashes, a somewhat sharp nose, and thin lips. She was twenty years of age when they married, her husband twenty-three. For the two years that Faruk went to secondary school in Izmir (he was to hang himself the summer of his graduation) he spent the winter in that house with his older sister, coming home only when the school year was out. Nebilé Hanim, on the occasional visits she made with Hashim Bey to see their two youngest, would implore, "Just once a month. You could hop the Thursday afternoon train and be back Friday evening." But Faruk would excuse himself with his studies. Summers—school ended in early June—the whole family would move to the Azmakaltı vineyards with the two watch towers. They would stay until the September grape harvest. After Faruk and his mother died the family managed to go only three more times. Fear of deserting troops kept them away during the mobilization, and throughout the Greek occupation there were robber bands to worry about. "Semra took it the hardest. She used to say summers had gone stale. Her first visit hadn't been much either, she was pregnant and couldn't ride. Maybe it was the day she wheedled Rüstem Bey into letting her mount up; at any rate, come fall her child was stillborn. The next summer they rode out almost every afternoon, coming in toward evening. I remember the sweaty horses, their flanks lathered. The coachman had to walk them before stabling them. Faruk generally went along, but would split off after a while so just the two of them could be alone. In fact there were days when he would rather have stayed behind, but then Semra always teased him; 'Young Law's afraid of losing,' and she'd laugh. Called him Young Law, for brother-in-law. One day he asked what made *her* that old. 'Four years,' she said, 'four whole years' difference, so.' Rüstem Abi would urge him to come along, too, 'Or I'll feel hurt.' Aunt Nebilé would pray after they left. One evening they were riding fast over a stubble field when Rüstem Abi's horse tripped and fell. Semra screamed. Faruk jumped off his mare before it even pulled up and ran with a cry, 'It's my fault,' to where Rüstem Abi lay on his stomach, deadly still with blood streaked across his forehead. Faruk sank down over him but Rüstem—he was playing possum—gave him a sudden hug and kiss. They came back together that dusk, trading jokes, laughing. The two brothers had always been close but after Rüstem Abi married, Faruk's love for him turned to adoration. He leapt to his every wish. And then the mare. One evening less than a week before he died Faruk was still out after dark and Aunt Nebilé got very worried. The men saddled up and went searching, Semra alongside her husband. They found him in the foothills beside an olive grove, guarding the mare he had ridden into the ground. 'I won't let the jackals get her,' he said. They roped her carcass to the other horses for the long haul back, and that night dug a ditch to bury her."

More and more cars were passing outside. The sound of a train reached him. You wondered what Faruk had been thinking as he rode his horse to death. Had that been the evening he came to the final choice? For him to cry out, "It's my fault" when his brother lay seemingly dead meant he had death in mind, and the guilt of it was on him. After the marriage Faruk's love had turned to worship. People thought he avoided his sister-in-law out of respect. No one had understood, unless perhaps Nebilé Hanim sensed something. Didn't Semra know either? She may have been so intent on Rüstem that her "Young Law's" furtive glances—at meals or out riding—went unnoticed. Since the couple, by his mother's account, used to slip down to the river on sultry nights, coming back toward morning, he must have sat by the window in the dark and waited. For his brother? On such nights Faruk himself apparently used to go out, but would return long before they did. Perhaps one night, when the heat kept him awake and he left his bed to go half-naked down to the river, he had seen them resting together or asleep on the small, tree-enclosed beach so that after, on torchlit evenings between the two "towers"—the ground having been sprinkled before sunset and spread with straw mats, the flat tin receptacles of kerosene-soaked charcoal aloft on four thick poles, and a banquet of dishes spread before them cooked by Chief Maid Kadriyé with the two servant girls (and which, under the watchful eye of his mother he forced himself to eat)—the meal over and conversation falling off he would withdraw to his room (else his mother would expect him back) and lie there till the flames were extinguished below and everyone had turned in; emerging then to go sit near that clearing by the river bank, aware of a fish or a frog or sliver of earth shearing off and splashing into the river, of the two watchdogs that barked in answer to a jackal's distant howl, of the evenly spaced hoots of an owl perched in a tree on the other bank—likely calling its mate—and uncertain in all the passing time why he waited; guilty, on edge, as he watched the moon- or starlight-outlined vines through which the two of them might soon again come down. Was that it? The two of them naked on those hot, breathless nights when even the screened open window gave no relief and sweat slicked their bodies where they touched, if one spoke—"They're all asleep now, let's go to the river"—and with sheets wrapped round them, moving cautiously in the dark so the household would sleep on, they stepped out into the cool air hand in hand, and barefoot, ignoring the bite of dirt clods, running over the freshly plowed rows between vines to reach the clearing and lie down, or perhaps they swam first, entwined wetly on the sheets then and joining; would he creep close enough to see, crawl up where he could hear their moans, their choked voices, her cry of "ahh, hold me always"? Or would he flee back to the tower? Hadn't he called the servant girl up one of those nights? A young girl whose hand trembled pouring the young bey his cup of water, who blushed when he looked at her—he must have asked her up one night toward the end, to find that only for one woman, for one woman impossible. . . . Zeberjet shook his head sharply. All this was conjecture, his own interpretation of hearsay. There was nothing to ensure that his mother hadn't exaggerated, even lied, in telling what she had seen and heard. And actually she hadn't referred to such an attachment. "We could never understand why he took his life at nineteen. He told no one, left behind not one small note. We went through his wardrobe, chest, books and diaries with a fine-toothed comb; but there was nothing." If Rüstem Bey had suspected Faruk of pining for his wife would he have named all his sons after him? When ten years following the suicide Rüstem Bey named his third boy, like the first two, Faruk, someone told him the name was a death sentence and he answered, "If he dies, it's with this name. He lives, still this name." Interpretation and hunting for motives didn't count, they yielded no certain answers. What counted was the act, and there was but one certainty after all for man.

Beyond the curtain it was no longer dark. The light that seeped through made objects distinguishable. The foot of the bed, the table, chair and kerosene stove, his clothes on the rack, the white lampshade that hung from the ceiling. Would it bear his weight eighteen days from now? Why was he waiting? The bed trembled. Would absurdity, contradiction, interruption become meaningful if they happened on November twenty-eighth?

He got up.

He dressed.

He made the bed.

He washed his face. A three-day stubble.

He brewed tea and drank two glasses.

The clock on the safe showed 8:15 when he sat down behind the desk. He opened the register. Since November 4th he had put down no names for imaginary clientele. Basically the running of a hotel was no different from running an institution, managing a large business, or governing a country. Just when you began to know yourself and understand what the means at hand might be, that's when you slipped and broke down. Luckily the managers of government didn't realize this, or they could do much more harm than the manager of a small hotel. He closed the register. What point was there any more in putting down these names, or leaving a note behind? Later a police report—minus the "questions put"—would establish that it all took place on November 4th. Suppose some thorough investigator examined the books and found that the people who stayed overnight between October 30th and November 4th last year had stayed again this year. On the very same days, in the very same rooms. What would he make of it? Zeberjet smiled. He rose and laid last year's register back in its chest under the stairs. From the drawer he took the key to Room 2. He saw the cloud-topped mountain on his way up, from the window on the landing. He returned from Room 2—the Retired Officer had spent a week there—with the clothesline left by those emissaries of the Veterinarian Bey. Back in his room again, he set the shaving kit at the base of the wall and drew the table over to the bed, lifting it up with some difficulty onto the mattress. He took off his shoes and socks. Jacket, slacks and sweater, at first draped over the chair, he re-hung on the rack. Getting onto the bed in his underwear he pushed down on the table, testing, then climbed carefully up and stood erect. He grasped the short length of lead pipe above the white lampshade and pulled down on it with both hands. With a cracking sound a chip of wood split off where the pipe joined the ceiling. Paint and plaster fell in his hair and face. He stepped down onto the bed and then the floor. The lampshade hung lopsided at the end of its pipe. Retrieving the clothesline from the foot of the bed he went to the pantry for the bread-knife and pestle, which he carried up to Room 2. There he pushed the bed—the foot first, then the head—over to the window. Pounding on the knife handle with the pestle in the middle of the floor he cut out a sizeable patch of linoleum. His face was drained of color now and grim, his breathing shallow. He leaned back against the bed and sat for a time regarding the worn, darkened boards he had exposed. They had found their way here decades ago and had been nailed in. It would have been woodcutter women who hewed them, in some forest on a mountain. Felled with axes and bucksaws by the men, lopped, debarked and left in the shade to dry, the great pine logs had lain in a clearing (on who knew what mountain—perhaps the Sabuncubeli forests) until the woodcutter women with their heavy *shalvars* (even on late, hot summer afternoons, while the men yawned in the woods or goat-hair tents and went to sleep and the goats themselves had left off foraging to seek the deep shade), with their multiple skirts, their

embroidered yellow red and black woolen vests and block-
print, beaded, sequin-fringed cotton scarves (stopping now
and again to wipe their brows as they called out "Zeeyy-
nep, haul that water!" and a little girl would hurry from the
tent, leaning to one side with the weight of a pine or juni-
per-wood jug—chiseled or carved out of a log, the water in
it sweet with the wood's fragrance—whose handle-less,
broad-mouthed form the women would raise, drops spill-
ing down their chins onto the swollen bust of their wool
vests) came along to wield the sharp, hot bucksaws, sun-
light flashing off them, sawing in the tenacious rhythm
needed to cut out the boards, which would then be packed
by mules (or hauled on a man's back) down to a foothill
road and the waiting oxcarts (those beasts slow and monu-
mental, the carts squealing as the great yoke-bowed necks
surged on the downhill—uphill they would strain with the
pointy stick goading their flanks) and on to the lumber
warehouses in town, where Malik Agha, his new manor
house going up, must have bargained and bullied them
away at the meanest rate, or had his construction foremen
procure them, to be brought and set in place here some one
hundred and twenty-five years ago. Zeberjet bent down,
and using the knife began to gouge at the wood. The boards
were all but rotten, soft with being worn down—before
the linoleum had been laid—by feet, slippers, clogs and
brooms; and with soaking up the water scrub-brushed and
rag-swabbed into them once a week (by a servant girl, the
pail beside her, rear end wagging as she retreated across the
floor on her knees, who had first taken up the rugs, felt
mats, carpets, and cushions—and who would one day be
married off with a paltry dowry, some poor relative [or
other stand-in, but poor] the aftermath of thorough use at
the hands of the household men: pinching at every

opportunity, the feeling up and then ducking—some went gladly, others had to be pulled—into a room, a bed); and soft too with the nightly audible gnawing of woodworms. He found he could do without the pestle, simply using the knife to chop with while the wood—especially where the rust-eaten nails were—crumbled away. Before long he had a hole and was looking down through it. It was near the place where the ceiling had broken when he yanked on the lead pipe. Chopping with the knife he enlarged the hole in that direction, then let one end of the rope down through both openings. Passing the other end over the bed he tied it underneath in the center, with repeated tight knots. On his feet again he pushed the bed back to the middle of the room, the head first, then the foot. The rope had laid a groove in the quilt. He pulled hard on it. Strong enough. Who could have made this bed, he wondered, when it had first been brought here? And who could have guessed the use it would someday be put to? He went downstairs with the knife and pestle. Setting the pestle down he opened the cupboard in the pantry to scoop a little shortening onto a small plate. This he took to his room, closing the door when he was inside. The rope, its one end going up through the ceiling, had slid off the table onto the bed, where it lay loosely coiled. He put the knife and plate on the table. Slowly, carefully keeping his balance, he climbed up. He gripped the rope and hauled on it with his entire weight. The knots held in the room above. Using the knife to saw at the rope he cut off a decent length, which he tossed over by the door together with the knife. He made a noose and running knot in the rope that hung, greased it, and tossed the plate down at the foot of the bed. It fell intact. Another faint vibration went through the table. Zeberjet put his head through the noose and adjusted it. At that moment several horns honked outside. These were joined by others, and then it was horns, train whistles and factory sirens in a long, unbroken blaring. What was this? Were his ears playing tricks on him? Or was it an appeal from the world outside? He was still here, everything was still in his control. He could slip the rope off, wait some more, run for it, give himself up, burn down the manor house. The freedom of choice was unbearable. He knocked the table over with a push of his feet; and falling through emptiness stopped short. Eyes and mouth open, legs stiffening and threshing, he reached up in an effort to grab the rope. (What came over him? Had he thought of something left undone? Or was it the parting realization that the gift of life is unparalleled and the one task on earth is to guard it, to hold out no matter what, to stay? Or was it the flesh in mute, mindless rejection fending off death? His head was sinking. His arms dangled. A thickish ivory fluid oozed from under his shorts and down the left leg. Catching in the hairs above his knee, it ran onto the quilt and spread. Above him the swinging rope made a creaking noise where it rubbed against the wood.

Yusuf Atilgan (1921-1989) was a Turkish novelist and dramatist, best known for his novels *Aylak Adam* (*The Flâneur*) and *Anayurt Oteli* (*Motherland Hotel*). A pioneer of the modern Turkish novel, Atılgan's work, in dealing with the existential crises of human beings, probes the depths of human psychology. His novel *Aylak Adam* was published in 1959, followed in 1973 by *Anayurt Oteli*, which gained further fame when a film based on the novel was made in 1987. Atılgan died of a heart attack in 1989 while in the middle of writing a novel titled *Canistan*, later published in incomplete form. Atılgan is also the author of a popular children's book and a collection of short stories.

Fred Stark was an American translator who resided in Turkey for many years. His translations include works from many of Turkey's most prominent authors, and commentary and interviews with cultural figures and artists. His translation of "The Mulberry Trees," constitutes the final section of Bilge Karasu's novel, *A Long Day's Evening* (City Lights, 2012), which was shortlisted for the PEN Translation Prize in 2013.